ON THE RIGHT TRACK

SAM KADENCE

Harmony Ink

Published by
Harmony Ink Press
5032 Capital Circle SW
Ste 2, PMB# 279
Tallahassee, FL 32305-7886
USA
publisher@harmonyinkpress.com
http://harmonyinkpress.com

On the Right Track
Copyright © 2013 by Sam Kadence

Cover Art by Aaron Anderson
aaronbydesign55@gmail.com

Cover content is being used for illustrative purposes only
and any person depicted on the cover is a model.

ISBN: 978-1-62798-069-2
Library ISBN: 978-1-62798-071-5
Digital ISBN: 978-1-62798-070-8

Printed in the United States of America
First Edition
August 2013

Library Edition
November 2013

CHAPTER 1

RU'S phone pinged with a new message from Tommy.

Looks like another one, sorry.

The text was attached to a photo of the cover of a magazine featuring Ru kissing his ex-boyfriend Kris and then a smaller picture of Kris kissing another guy. Headline for that one was Vocal Growth Star Jilted! Six months and still front page news.

He sighed. Even leaving California hadn't helped. Here he was in the cold autumn of Minnesota, alone, but still stalked by the conservative media who thought anyone under eighteen didn't deserve to recognize their sexuality. Sure he was gay. He'd known for years. Had even made the mistake of telling his father when he was eleven. Why did that make him a bad guy?

As part of a boy band that had traveled the world a few times and won a hefty number of awards, he was required to maintain a wholesome image. At least that's what his former recording studio had told him. And wholesome didn't mean kissing another guy, even when he and Kris had been exclusive for almost two years. So, while it was okay for other celebrities to come out and show pride, anyone under the magical age of eighteen was ridiculed, cast out, and treated as a pariah of the community.

Do you need me to come stay with you? Tommy texted again. He was a former bandmate but still a good friend. Tommy hadn't cared when Ru told him he was gay. He did offer to kick the crap out of Kris after the guy had set them up to be photographed together, outing Ru to the whole world, only to then cheat on him. Would Ru's heart ever stop breaking at the memory?

Ru texted back *He never really loved me, did he?*

A second later the phone rang. Ru answered it, knowing who the voice on the other line would be. "I'm on my way to the airport," Tommy said.

"You don't have to come all the way out here for me. I'm fine. Virtually unrecognized here." Though Ru hadn't done much other than venture to his Uncle Dimitri's restaurant. He was sure he would put on ten pounds before the week was over. "I'm just laying low. Trying to work on some music."

"And still not over that bastard Kris."

Maybe. But that part of his life had ended. In fact, so much had changed that Ru found himself more lost and depressed than he had most of his life. He'd always known exactly who he was and what he wanted. He'd never been more alive than when he was on stage, surrounded by cheering fans and bright lights. His very Asian father had pushed him to become the musician he was with years of piano and guitar lessons, high-end tutors, and business sense. Ru found passion in the music and had made himself famous, trusting his dad to always be there. Only that hadn't happened. And Ru had been on his own a while now. Still loving the music and building his life around the fame he'd crafted. But now he wasn't so sure about it all. The constant flash of the camera, the endless judgment of strangers, and the never-ending loneliness, was that all that was left for him? Was that what he'd worked so hard and given up his childhood for? "I don't want to talk about that."

"Okay, so tell me how your meeting with the big M went."

Ru smiled. "She was amazing. Probably had no clue who I was, but it was good." His publicist, Katie, had arranged the meeting to try to bolster Ru's spirit. The woman was a miracle worker, but even meeting his idol could only lift him for a little while.

"You been working on any new songs? I don't know what we're going to do without you writing them all for us in the group." What Tommy didn't say was that AJ, another bandmate, was already on the search for a new guy to add to the ranks of Vocal Growth, as Ru had been released from the group when he'd been outed. "Released" was a nice term used in the media to make it sound like he'd had a choice.

"Haven't really been inspired."

"I'll be there in a few hours. Maybe we can hit the clubs or something."

"It's really cold here. You know that, right?" Ru couldn't imagine wearing most of his club clothes out in this weather. He'd have to find some fancy coat that would cover it all just to keep from freezing his nuts off. "How do you go clubbing in Eskimo gear?"

"It's what, fifty degrees? You big baby. Just wait until January. See you in a few hours. Maybe go to Dimitri's or something. I don't want you home alone."

They hung up, and Ru glared at the picture of the magazine cover. He dialed the driver he'd hired, left the borrowed apartment—Tommy's, actually—and headed out, unsure of where he would go. Anywhere had to be better than alone. Binks opened the car door for him, though Ru had told him a hundred times it wasn't necessary. God, it was so cold here.

"Where would you like to go, sir?" Binks asked.

"I want to go somewhere there are people, but where no one will recognize me. Not shopping or whatever. I don't know." He needed to get to a bookstore and find something to read. He'd forgotten his book reader in San Diego. But a bookstore meant people who would want photos and autographs or even point and stare. Libraries had books, but he didn't think he'd ever been in one. His homeschool instructor had issued him a MNSCU—Minnesota State Colleges and Universities—pass, which allowed access to almost any library in the state. "Is there a good library around here? Not a public one—too many people—maybe a college one?"

"Would you like to stay in the city or head to the suburbs? The suburbs will likely be less crowded."

True enough. "Anything near Dimitri's?" Tommy had been right. He didn't want to be by himself. Maybe he'd stop in to see his uncle for dinner. God knew the man treated him more like a son than Ru's own father ever had. Though Ru still hadn't seen his uncle since his outing had happened.

"Yes, I know of the perfect place," Binks said, and off they went.

Ru paid very little attention to the scenery they passed. The trees were pretty, all colors, and skies mostly clear. He should have felt inspired, but he hadn't written a note since arriving almost two weeks ago, and it worried him. Usually the music came easily; he'd just sit down and there it was. But ever since Kris—well, their breakup, if a public outcry could be called a breakup—he hadn't written a damn thing. How many times had Kris called, asking to talk to him, begging for forgiveness? Ru just felt numb. The months ignoring him made it hurt less, but the media never seemed to let it die. So he'd fled. Run from his warm and usually welcoming home in San Diego, where all his friends were, to Minnesota, and the quiet downtown apartment Tommy owned.

To be honest, Ru had lost a lot of friends. Not because they hadn't known he was gay. Everyone in his circle had been well aware of the fact. No, people stopped calling him because he was in disgrace. The record label threw him out; his bandmates pretended he didn't exist, except Tommy; and his former friends had moved on to whoever could get them into the parties with the brightest and most popular celebrities.

The more he thought about it, the more heartbreaking it became. Not just losing Kris, but realizing that all the people Ru had considered his makeshift family had really just been playing him. How was anyone supposed to get past that?

Staying downtown put him near all the clubs, live music, and a handful of private production studios he could rent. Tommy's apartment had a small studio built in just for late-night jam sessions. Ru had already signed contracts to record a solo album, his true lifelong dream, with another record label. His new producer didn't care he was gay and was unwilling to go back into the closet. Ru's voice spoke for itself, and his songwriting was legendary. Yet, since that day almost six months ago, he felt so empty.

Tommy suggested Ru spend time away from the spotlight. Ru remembered the conversation pretty well.

"You're so young, Ru. Maybe just get away for a while. Find yourself."

"Who even says that?" Ru groused, irritated by his best friend treating him with kid gloves. At least Tommy had remained his friend.

"The guy who's watched you grow up a music machine. Don't forget I saw how your dad pushed you, and then, when he left, it was like you were hell-bent on making yourself a brighter star than he'd ever imagined, just to show him up." Tommy took out a suitcase and began packing Ru's stuff. "I think you need some time to figure out who Ryunoski Nakimura really is. Not the guy on the cover of magazines, but the guy with the wide smile and shy heart."

Ru sighed. "You sound like a Hallmark card. Where am I supposed to go? In case you haven't noticed, the whole world knows who I am."

"They know who you show them you are. I'm not even sure I know who you are." Tommy waved away Ru's protest. "Don't get pissy with me. You can go to my flat in Minnesota. The town is pretty quiet but big. Sort of like a mini-New York without all the paps. We'll just make sure no one knows you've gone there. Even if people recognize you, they'd be really nice about it. It's what they call 'Minnesota Nice.'"

"Isn't it snowy there?"

"In late September? No. Sometimes you'll see a bit of snow in October, but nothing really sticks till December. And if you're still there, you can go skiing. You like skiing."

"I liked sitting by the fire with Kris when we went to Denver. I hate the cold."

Tommy reached over and pulled Ru into a hug. "I don't think you realize the tone in your voice when you say his name. It's like your heart breaks each time. You can't keep living like this, seeing him at promo stuff or parties…."

"No one invites me to parties anymore." Ru had gone from being on the top of everyone's list to not even existing. The depression was really starting to eat at him.

"That's why it's a good time to go. Find some new scenery, maybe even some new friends. People who won't judge you by how many magazines you're in or how many awards you've won." Tommy sighed. "Do you have any idea how much it hurts me to see you so lost? You're like my kid brother, and the world just took a dump on your head. So now I want to beat up the whole fucking world."

"Not good for your image."

Tommy squeezed tighter for a moment before letting go and returning to packing. "I don't care about that. Life isn't all about the image you project to the world. I just want you to heal a little. So pack, please, and forget about Kris. He didn't deserve you."

And so Ru had made his way to the Twin Cities, Minnesota, hoping, just a little, for a chance to restart. When he really thought about it, he realized he'd never really loved Kris. Sure, he'd liked the man well enough. Kris had been kind and good-looking. He knew lip service like few others, but that's all it had really been. He knew exactly what to say to get Ru to agree to just about anything. Only now did Ru look back and realize it was because he'd been affection-starved after his father left. He'd thrown himself at Kris to fill the gap in his soul that Tommy couldn't seal alone. Ru had tried to use Kris. And so, in kind, Kris had used Ru.

Kris wanted Ru's fame, and without any talent of his own, figured using Ru to get it was what he needed; thus the career-ending picture. Well, maybe not career-ending, but it sure felt that way at the time. The phone calls never stopped, flashes of thousands of cameras, people screaming things about him being damned. Even fans abandoning him because he was obviously "perverted" and "evil." Ru had never imagined that by seventeen he'd be the world's biggest scandal. What would they all think if they knew AJ lip-synced at almost every concert because the guy couldn't dance and sing at the same time? Or that Dane was about as sharp as a box of river rocks? How had him being born gay made him such a bad guy?

The car pulled up to a small community college, ripping Ru out of his brooding. Next door to it was an even smaller high school. Ru recognized them only because Binks described it to him. In his part of California, the schools were all a mass of tiny buildings, each classroom its own little freestanding structure. Here they were like massive apartments attached by tunnels above and below ground. Sort of like the way schools looked like on TV, only with fewer windows. Cooled for the warm summer months and heated for the wicked cold Ru already felt coming. Several floors and long hallways of classrooms lined with lockers—it just all seemed so odd to him.

Binks opened the door and waved his hand to a building on the right. "That's the library. Three floors, great selection of music titles as well as current fiction, and only about ten minutes from Dimitri's. Do you want me to tell your uncle you'll be coming by for dinner?"

Ru shook his head. "Nah. I'll tell him when I get there. Stay close, please." He headed into the library, marveling at the walls of windows and towering stacks of books. Everything was numbered, so

Ru had to stop at the information desk to ask for directions to the music section. Once the librarian had pointed him in the right direction, he wove his way through the stacks, reading through titles until he found a few books to browse. For a community college, they had a really large section on music.

There were people everywhere, many sitting at tables or on computers. A handful of students had even gathered around a large fireplace in the center of the library, acoustic guitars in hand, playing and singing softly. No one rushed to shush them, and everyone really just seemed intent on minding their own business. Ru made his way to a table near the back, next to one of the giant windows, and set down his stack of books.

The view was nice. There was some sort of courtyard area outside with benches, trees, and even a few pergola-looking things. Rainbows of leaves lay scattered about, and he wondered how peaceful it would look when it was all blanketed in the white of winter. He'd done the ski-trip thing a few times with Tommy, but had a feeling that actually living here during the winter months would be a world of differences.

Finally he just sighed and opened a book. The noise of the people around him was comforting and eased him out of his depression, though he couldn't really interact with them. He hoped just keeping his head down would be enough to prevent anyone from recognizing him.

He was halfway through a biography about Madonna when he heard someone sit down at a desk nearby. Somewhat afraid he'd been discovered, Ru looked up. The young man had the blondest hair he'd ever seen on a guy, which was saying a lot since Ru was born and raised in San Diego. But it was a fine, white shag that fell around his face. The guy's profile was lovely, all angles until the softness of his lips broke it up. Ru must have been staring too long because the blond glanced his way.

Ru buried his face back in his book, trying to slow his excited breathing. The kid was beautiful. Giant brown eyes, soft and sweet, lips thick and expressive, skin so oddly pale and light brown all at once. He looked so innocent, not that Ru could think of why that was. It was just that he didn't appear to be the kind of guy he'd been used to, the hangers-on in designer clothes and makeup. Wholesome, the boy-next-door type of guy Ru had been hearing about his entire life. They were probably pretty close in age. For the first time in ages, Ru actually felt something more than sadness, depression, and rage.

Hope.

Their eyes met briefly, and the blond smiled shyly at him. Ru ran his hands through his brown hair a few times. It felt coarse and unappealing, just like he did at that moment. What sort of other life would he have to live to end up with a boy like this? Did this pretty boy struggle every day to put forth such a perfect image? Or could he just be who he was?

They played the game a while, glancing up or looking away when the other looked up. Ru licked his lips more times than usual trying to find the voice to speak up and actually introduce himself to the young man. The guy's clothes were normal, just T-shirt and jeans, with a light coat, nothing that said he was a pap or anything other than the student he appeared to be. But Ru found himself locked in his seat, not sure what to say or how to react each time the kid looked up.

The blond got up after a few minutes, leaving his books and everything to head to the counter. Ru watched him talk to the librarian for a minute before rushing to find a piece of paper to leave the young man a note. What if the guy had heard of him? What if he was disgusted and turned around and called the papers or something? What if Ru spent the rest of his life wondering what if?

He jotted down just his nickname and his phone number. Maybe the guy would call; maybe he wouldn't. At least Ru had made his move. He headed into the stacks, hoping the guy didn't come barreling after him shouting hateful things when he found the note, but he stayed close enough to watch.

The young man returned with a handful of papers. He frowned, glanced at where Ru had sat a minute ago, and opened his folder. Ru knew he'd found the note by the alarmed expression on the blond's face. He even looked up and glanced around as if afraid someone would see him. He seemed to be confused by the note. Ru felt his heart break a little and turned to leave, texting Binks as he went. So much for hope.

CHAPTER 2

ADAM'S high school campus shared libraries with the local community college, which would have been cool if the large cavernous space hadn't been somewhat intimidating to the average guy like him. It wasn't that he did badly in school. His grades were pretty good. He even liked to read. It was just that the library was swarming with college students. The reason he had to visit the library that day was simply because he had a paper to write, and his parents had so restricted the Internet access at home he couldn't find anything on the topic he'd decided to write about.

He wandered through the rows of books and filled computer stations until he found a free computer near the back. Someone sat kitty-corner at an open desk, nose buried in a book. The guy had nice shoulders, even though they were hunched. His hands rested in his dark hair, face mostly hidden, but Adam allowed himself a nice once-over. He'd gotten good at admiring from a distance. The guy was probably a college kid, since Adam didn't recognize him from any of his classes.

Adam spared him one last glance before sitting down to do a few searches. With less than an hour before practice, he had a lot to do. Probably fifteen minutes had passed when he felt that weird itching down his spine telling him someone was watching him. He glanced up and met the startled pale-blue gaze of the dark-haired guy. The guy glanced back to his book guiltily. Adam hid a small smile. He wondered if the guy was straight. Adam wasn't out since, at sixteen, that was social suicide, but he was well aware of where his preferences lay. A look didn't mean much, and he'd never really had anyone look at him, but he couldn't help but glance the guy's way a few more times.

Now that Adam could see his profile, he was stunned by how the guy looked. Like some sort of celebrity—perfect skin, thick lips, endless lashes, and thick brows that blended well with his shaggy hair. The young man's eyes had a slight slant, but were wide and blue. Mousy brown hair fell around the edges of his face. Adam fought to keep from staring at the guy. He'd glance up, and Adam would look away. It was a game he enjoyed for a while as he searched halfheartedly for information on how interracial couples sought and won marriage equality. The topic had sounded interesting when his English professor, Mrs. Saudi, had handed the class a list of suggestions for controversial topics. But that had been before Pretty Blue Eyes had glanced his way.

He wondered what had brought the guy into the library that day, and if Adam would have seen him if only he visited the library more. Sure, Adam admired some of the college guys from afar since they all shared a parking lot, and he saw his fair share. But none of them looked at him the way this guy had. And none of them set a weird feeling turning in his stomach, some kind of odd mix of fear and excitement. What would happen if they actually spoke to each other? Would Adam even know what to say? Would a guy like that even be willing to listen?

Though Adam regretted having to move, he probably had a stack of stuff clogging up the printer. Leaving his spot for a minute to retrieve them, he hoped the hot guy would still be there when he got back, and maybe Adam would even talk to him.

He went to the counter. "I'm Adam Corbin. I have some printouts to pick up," he told the woman behind the desk. She patted her gray poufy hair and looked around confused for a moment before realizing the printer was right behind her. All high school stuff went to that printer. The college kids had to pay for their own stuff, so they had a wall of printers they had to log into to print.

She handed Adam a stack of papers, and he dug out what was his, returned the rest, then headed back to the computer. The guy was gone. Adam sighed sadly. The guy had left his stack of books on the table; music books and biographies about musicians. Three about Madonna. Okay, so maybe the guy was gay. Did straight guys like Madonna?

Wasn't there some unwritten rule that you had to be gay or female to like her?

Adam opened his folder to stick the printed articles inside and a slip of folded paper sat there. Unfolding it with nervous hands, he darted a glance around to see who might be watching, but saw no one. The paper just said "Ru" and a phone number. He probably stood there for several minutes gaping like a fish at those beautifully etched numbers, both terrified and hopeful. His first thought was to ask himself how the guy had known Adam might be interested. Had there been too much in the glance? Was it the way he talked or walked? What about the way he dressed?

Only one guy in school was out, and he was way out, wore heels and makeup. He had an undeniable swish to his hips and that awful lisp Adam feared would somehow develop if he came out. Bas was also one of the smartest guys in school, so he really hid nothing. They had been friends in junior high until Adam started noticing he liked boys in the way most other guys liked girls. Then when Bas came out, he'd followed the crowd and kept his distance, fearing what everyone else would do if he didn't.

Adam did a lot to fit in. He played sports he didn't care for, like football. He was small and fast and ran on the track team. He wasn't a braincase or a jock. He was sort of a middle-of-the-road guy. But he worked hard not to stand out. With a year and a half until graduation, he had hoped to continue to coast until the final bell rang.

He remembered when Bas came out and the beating the man had received. Only then had Adam stepped up and starting pushing people back when they shoved him. He had seen firsthand what the other kids could do to you if you let them. But he was nowhere near brave enough to be out like Bas was, even if he'd been inclined that way.

The panic began to fade as he headed toward the locker room and practice. Maybe the guy hadn't known. Maybe he was just hoping. Hell, Adam was trying to make a plan to call him and be nonchalant about it. Every day he was surrounded by guys, some really good-looking, but none who really interested him. There was a difference between knowing you liked guys and actually finding someone around exciting enough to risk social isolation.

In the locker room, where guys walked around almost naked most of the time, Adam had looked the first few times, but pretty was pretty and that's it. None of them did anything for him. Which he guessed was good, since popping wood around a crowd of guys twice his size would probably end up with him getting his ass kicked. Other boys talked about girls and awkwardly about sex, yet he found himself walking away whenever the conversations began. Did that make him different? Was that because he was gay? Surely gay guys were interested in sex by sixteen too? So why wasn't he?

He changed into track pants and slipped a long-sleeved running shirt over a clean tank; late September was not known for warmer temperatures in Minnesota. Soon the snow would come, and then he'd be stuck indoors, which was never as peaceful as a full-out run through fresh air. Still, all he could think about were those stunning pale-blue eyes.

Ru. What sort of name was Ru?

After programming the number into his phone, he just stared at it for a while, unconscious of everyone around leaving the locker room until the coach called him. "Corbin, you playing today or too busy daydreaming?"

"Sorry, sir. I'm coming." Adam stuffed everything into his locker and quickly tied his shoes before heading out to the field. Maybe running a few miles would get his mind off the blue-eyed stranger whose phone number was taunting him.

The coach made all the guys who played football run, even the linebackers, who were obviously born to tackle people because they were so wide they had to turn sideways to fit through doorways. They lumbered along behind everyone, barely above a walking pace, while Adam set his pace at a pretty solid run. Nate and Jonah kept up pretty well. If it came down to a sprint, he'd have them both beat, even though they were taller. Nate was quarterback and one of the most popular guys in school. He had odd, dusty-brown hair and piercing blue eyes that made him look like the most likely to end up someone important. And while Adam found him nice to look at, he hadn't bothered to get too close because Nate had enough hangers-on who liked to torment others, and Adam had no desire to be one of the popular kids or the most beat on kids. Jonah was Nate's number one hanger-on. Adam, he was just a teammate, and grateful most days to be that.

"We're going to State," Nate said, breath still solid. They'd all have to go more than a few miles to really be working up the sweat the coach wanted. A half an hour of running, then off to drills. Though of late, Nate had been requesting more time on the track.

"Of course we are. With you as our quarterback, we can't be beat," Jonah piped up.

"I mean for track." Nate looked at Adam.

Adam glanced in Nate's direction with a raised brow. Nate was fast, but he wasn't beating anyone in regionals; too much bulk and not enough leg to make up for it. They had six months to work toward it, but since last year, they hadn't even made it to regionals. He didn't hold out much hope for this year.

"Means you, Corbin." Jonah nudged the smaller man. "You're the fastest shit around."

Why did that sound like a bad thing coming from him? "I cannot take us to State by myself." Track didn't work that way anymore than football did.

"No I in team, eh?" Nate teased. He nodded back toward the stands. "Friend of yours?"

"Huh?" They didn't really have anyone who watched when they ran unless it was an actual competition, because, well, running in circles wasn't really all that exciting. In fact, football drills were sort of boring in general. Adam glanced back toward the stands, and on the end near the fence was the pretty, blue-eyed guy from the library. "Crap."

Adam stumbled but recovered quickly enough to catch up to Nate and Jonah again and not kill himself trying. His face burned with embarrassment from almost wiping out in front of Ru, who he really didn't know at all but somehow cared more about than the two guys he'd attended school with for years.

"No, I don't know him," Adam denied and put all his focus into moving his feet.

They ran drills for almost two hours. Nate requested more course time from the coach, who agreed and then told Adam and Jonah to join him. The backers gave up halfway through, pretending to tackle each other or just sitting on the bench. Even Jonah gave up, but Nate seemed determined to keep going, even though both he and Adam were breathing hard. Adam was in the zone, had thrown off the long-sleeved top, leaving just a tank, and let the chill evening air cool his heated skin. He could have gone for hours, the burn in his lungs familiar, his legs and thighs pushing hard in rhythmic strides. They weren't even going that fast. But he'd rather run than play tackle dummy.

When the coach blew the whistle and told them to head to the showers, Adam slowed to a walk and finished two more laps, stretching to keep his muscles from seizing up. Nate followed his lead, but shook his head at the group of guys eager to get away from the course and into the showers.

"No devotion. We're never going to win with a team like this."

Adam retrieved his shirt and a clean towel. "Not everyone likes to run. And the guys do okay with knocking each other down. That's sort of the point of football." Until Adam had discovered how peaceful it could be a little over a year ago, he had hated running.

"The U is offering scholarships for runners. I think they want more variety with the Gophers 'cause they've been sucking so bad this year. They were so busy picking the biggest, scariest guys they could find they forgot they had to have guys who could actually move." Nate stretched and patted Adam on the shoulder. "I'm sure we could all use some scholarship money."

Ah, so that was why he was all hyped on the track thing. Not that it mattered, since Adam didn't plan on attending the U of M. He honestly had no idea what he wanted to do with the rest of his life. He just knew he wanted it to be something else, somewhere else. But it made sense why Nate would work so hard. He was a senior. Adam was just a junior and was actually looking into going to an out-of-state school, maybe something in Washington or Maine, where it wasn't always about sports or being the top of the class.

Wiping the sweat off his face and shoulders as they made their way back to the locker room, Adam scanned the stands looking for Ru. He was gone. Adam sucked in a heavy sigh and headed back to the showers. Probably best Ru didn't see him covered in sweat and stinking. No one would find that attractive.

THE next week Adam stared at that number in his phone probably a hundred times a day without finding the courage to actually call. It wasn't until he was in study hall on Tuesday, cramming for the French test, that he actually thought about doing anything other than just thinking about it. Adam had almost hit the dial button when Sebastian "Bas" Axelrod, the flighty, out, gay guy, plunked into the seat next to him, all glitter and smiles. Their study hall meetings weren't unusual. He was in AP French and helped a lot of students out with their homework, Adam included.

"Adam, sweetie, you've been looking so distracted this week. Need some help preparing for the midterm?" He waved his hand at Adam's French book. "Maybe something to take your mind off whatever bug has gotten into your bonnet."

Adam couldn't help but laugh. Where did Bas get those lines? "I just need to practice my verbs. I'm more worried about the oral exam than the written part." It always made more sense on paper. He didn't know why.

"Oh, honey, I can help you with oral anytime."

Adam felt himself flush at Bas' teasing. And it was teasing. Bas did it every time they saw each other, and he did it to everyone. Adam didn't know if Bas had gaydar and could tell that he was gay as well, but Adam never felt he aimed more teasing at him than anyone else, so it was okay. "If you can help me with my French, I'd really appreciate it." The words were out of his mouth before he even realized Bas would probably pull a double meaning out of them too.

"Oh baby, I knew you'd come around. I'd love to help you French. Nothing sexier than that pretty platinum blond hair of yours or those big lips. OMG! Let's begin now." He pursed his lips dramatically.

Adam groaned. "Bas, behave, or I won't study with you anymore."

Bas gave Adam a huge dramatic sigh. "So beautiful, but so mean. So dish, sweetie, what's really on your mind?"

Bas was known for gossiping, so Adam hesitated to tell him anything. A quick glance around the room showed him everyone was occupied with other things and not paying attention to them. "So I saw this person in the library. And they were pretty attractive, even gave me their number, but I've been too scared to call."

"I see, said the sharply dressed gay man. Okay, so if you're worried about calling, text this hottie before she slips away."

Adam blinked at him. "Text?"

"Don't give me that deer-in-the-headlights look, sweetie, though it is absolutely breathtaking on you. I know you know how to text. Even you pretty runner types know how to put your thumbs together and pound out a message."

"The jock jokes are getting old." Adam picked up his phone and glanced at the screen again. Yeah, he could text Ru. That wasn't as scary as outright calling him.

Bas put his hands up in an "I'm harmless" sort of way. "Don't bite the messenger, baby. Nate has been hanging around you a lot, so I'm hearing a lot of the jock banter thrown around with your name attached. Some of the jockstraps are starting to get jittery." The "jockstraps" were his affectionate term for all Nate's hangers-on.

Adam frowned. Nate had been running with him every day, requesting Adam to stay late after football practice and just run. They'd even raced a few times, with the results being hands down that Adam was just faster than Nate. It probably bothered him, though it was all body structure rather than actual skill. Nate was built like a football player: thick, strong, and wide. Adam was built more like a swimmer: lean, lanky, and long-legged. "Nate is trying to get a scholarship to the U of M."

"Yeah, he sure isn't going to get one based on his grades. You, on the other hand, with a little work, could. You'd have better grades if you'd just apply yourself." He flung his hands about. "Stop being all wishy-washy."

"I'm not going to the U of M." Everyone at Northern High went to the U of M. It was like some sort of unspoken rule. If you went to college, and not just a community college like the one next door, you went to the U of M. Which was exactly why Adam wasn't going.

"All righty, then. On that somewhat incensed note, let's practice your French, shall we? Afterward you can text your Ms. Right and talk about moving to some grand place that doesn't snow eight months out of the year and accepts exceedingly unmotivated individuals like yourself." And just like that, he turned his focus to helping Adam learn instead of teasing him to death.

Adam spent a good part of that night after practice trying to figure out what exactly to text. In the end, he almost caved to the internal pressure and didn't send anything at all, but he shot off a quick text right before dinner that said *Hey, this is Adam, the guy from the library. So you're a Madonna fan?* An hour later he stared at the text in horror, realizing he'd pretty much asked the guy if he was gay in his first text to him. He probably wouldn't write back, and since it had been an hour already with no reply, Adam figured that was that. And it had been over a week, so the guy probably forgot ever having seen him. Who knows? Maybe the guy gave out his number to lots of other guys in libraries. He sighed, glaring at the phone.

"Adam?" his mom called from downstairs.

"Yeah?" he called back through his semiopen bedroom door.

"Do you need a ride to school tomorrow? Your dad has to work early."

"Nah, Mom. I'll walk, it's not that far." Really only five blocks, and since it wasn't snowing yet, it wasn't a big deal. Adam wondered if he should look for a part-time job over the holidays. Something to save up for a car, since he could legally drive now. But that would take time away from sports and school in general. Bas was right that he lacked direction. Everyone talked about college or what jobs they would have, but not him. He sighed and sat down on his bed with his laptop to finish the paper he'd started a week ago. Maybe when he was finished, he'd do some journaling and work out some of the confused meandering in his head.

After several hours of writing, Adam ended up crawling into bed around eleven, set his phone on the nightstand, and stared at it. No reply. He turned off the light and flipped over in bed, pulling the blanket over his head. Yeah, he was an idiot. See hot guy, piss off hot guy, live alone forever. He fell asleep thinking about it and had dreams about Ru walking right by him as he went off to kiss Bas instead.

CHAPTER 3

"STARING at the phone isn't going to make him call," Tommy pointed out. He set a plate down and shoved it Ru's way—steamed veggies and lean proteins.

Ru sighed. Why couldn't he just have pizza? Did he look like he'd already put on weight? AJ had spent years ragging on him about his weight, complaining he was too heavy to dance right and looked like a cow in the pictures they all took together, that it said bad things about the band. Ru had really begun to hate food.

"You need to eat." Tommy ran his hands through his messy brown hair and glared at the food too. "Yeah, okay. It's pretty bland. But it's healthy. Binks says you haven't been eating right, and you have a show tonight."

Binks needed to mind his own business. "I'm not really that hungry anyway."

"Just 'cause this boy you saw hasn't called?"

"He looked upset that I gave him my number. Of course he hasn't called. He was probably straight. I bet he thought I was a pervert or something, staring at him all that time."

"He smiled at you."

"You smile at me all the time," Ru pointed out.

Tommy rewarded him with one of his million-dollar smiles. "And I'm straight, so that makes him straight? No, most straight guys don't smile at other straight guys they don't know. We just sort of nod, like 'What's up,' and move on." He demonstrated the move.

"Then why hasn't he called? It's been over a week," Ru complained, cutting into the chicken. "He was better-looking than me."

"And you're probably more talented than him. Maybe you read the look wrong. Maybe he was smiling at someone else?" He nudged Ru's shoulder. "Maybe your gaydar is broken."

"Screw you. I caught him staring at me, and then he smiled." Ru groaned. "Oh man, that smile. Those lips. And do you have any idea how bad I want to run my hands through that hair? I wonder how soft it is. Do you think it could naturally be that shade? He'd have to have a really good colorist otherwise."

"What if he's a college kid?"

Ru shrugged. The guy hadn't looked that old, plus when he'd followed the kid to the football field, it had been on high school grounds. Northern High. Tommy didn't know much about it since it was a suburban school, and he'd lived downtown his whole life. Ru wished he'd been smart enough to get a picture before he'd left. Even with only a week gone by, he was having a hard time remembering the exact shade of the young man's pale blond hair and the soft clarity of his light-brown complexion. And those lips. God.

Ru sat up and tried to shift around in the chair enough to ease the sudden tightening in his pants. *Damn.* "You should have seen his skin, and those bow-shaped lips."

"Not really my deal. Don't suppose you got his name or anything?"

"Yeah, 'cause I'm gonna walk up to random people and ask, 'Hey, anyone know that hot blond kid who was here last week?'" Ru glared at his friend.

"You followed him out to the field. Didn't anyone call out to him? Or the teacher address him or anything?"

The truth was that Ru had been hypnotized by the way the kid ran. And even though watching him run with the two hulking football players had been like a bucket of ice water tossed at him, Ru had a hard time thinking of anything else since. If he'd been braver he'd have waited around until the guy was headed to the locker room and then approached. Maybe even asked for a date. But Kris had killed that confidence in him, made him this horribly cautious and bitter man. "I don't remember."

"You were just too busy looking at his ass."

And his legs, and his shoulders. The guy had been all sleek muscle. "He's probably a jerk anyway. All jocks are, you said so yourself," Ru pointed out. Tommy was twenty and had actually been in regular public schools most of his life, at least until the last four years of fame had ripped him out of it.

"Jocks don't go to the library for any reason. They bully nerds into doing that for them. I can't believe you didn't get any pictures of him on your phone." Ru's expression must have said not nice things because Tommy held up his hands. "I just mean for you to remember him by. Have you thought about going back to the school?"

"I've had enough experience with stalkers in my life to not want to do that to someone else."

"Kris still calling?" Tommy asked. Ru knew how he felt as Tommy had always been a pretty vocal guy.

"Only every few days or so. He leaves long rambling messages about how we need to get back together and how stupid he's been."

"He means his fame is fading so he needs another jolt."

"I guess."

"I *know*. So if you haven't forgotten, you're doing that LGBT benefit show in like two hours. Remember, embrace the out and proud. Time to get ready." Tommy checked his phone. "Binks is waiting downstairs with the car. So either finish eating your veggies or let's go get you decked out in official Ryunoski Nakimura style."

"Gay slut it is," Ru grumbled, pushing the food aside.

Tommy punched him in the arm. "Don't say crap like that." He took the tray and dragged Ru into the bedroom to begin the intensive process of choosing a wardrobe for the evening. Two hours, five clothing changes, and a bunch of makeup later, Ru was on point for a solo performance benefiting LGBT youth. He sang a couple of covers and did a few songs that Vocal Growth was known for in more of a rock style than the pop format most people were used to. Oddly enough, the show was sold out—almost four thousand in attendance.

And though he hadn't done much practicing in the past few weeks, Ru felt he sounded pretty good and was thrilled to not have to dance.

The pictures he took with people all seemed legit, some shaking his hand or wanting autographs. No one mentioned his fall from grace. One young man hugged him, muttering, "Thank you, thank you, thank you."

Ru patted his back and whispered comforting things to him, just believing the kid to be some overzealous fan.

"You coming out changed everything for me," the kid sobbed. Instantly Ru felt uncomfortable, but the kid wasn't letting go. "When my folks kicked me out, I spent so much time on the streets. Was selling myself just to eat. Didn't want to go to a shelter because they make you go to school, and at school people just bully you and beat you up. But it got so bad I just wanted to die. And then there you were. On the front page of every magazine. Ryunoski Nakimura, heartthrob to the whole world, child prodigy, and homosexual. All I could think of was, well, if he could do it, if he could make it, even when the whole world is saying bad things, I can't give up, you know? God made this beautiful, talented man, and made him gay too. He has to have a plan for me."

Ru sucked in a deep breath, not knowing what to say.

"Now I'm in a shelter for LGBT youth. They got me the ticket for this, and I'm in school. Gonna graduate no matter what. Going to help kids like us. Maybe become a psychologist or something. And it's all because of you."

"Thank you for telling me," Ru said, overwhelmed by the boy's gratitude. "But you have to do these things for yourself."

"Oh, I am! And screw that Kris Turlington guy. He's an ass and didn't deserve you anyway. I can't wait for your solo album. I bet you're going to blow Vocal Growth out of the water. Those guys are nothing without you."

Ru was again at a loss for words. He felt his phone vibrate, telling him he had a text. He ignored it, thinking it was probably just Kris bugging him again. The kid called over some of his friends, who had their own stories to tell him about how he'd been an inspiration to them, still was an inspiration to them. For the first time in six months, Ru felt like maybe things were going to be okay.

Over the next couple of days, Ru flew around the country doing exactly the same thing: performing for LGBT youth and trying to raise awareness and funds to help the kids. At every event there was a line of kids wanting to tell him their stories. Ru wrote two songs in the midst of all that madness, on the plane or in the dressing room, stuff about not giving up and pain not being enough for him to let go of it all. Tommy accompanied him to almost all the shows, though by now he had AJ on his ass screaming at him to come back to San Diego so they could finish choosing the guy who would replace Ru.

"You should just go," Ru told Tommy. "He's only going to get angrier the longer he waits."

"He's going to pick a replacement with or without me there. Just as they all agreed to kick you out without asking my opinion. And so you know, Dane had no part in that either. That was AJ and the record label. And between you and me, I'm pretty sure it was just because AJ felt you were getting more attention than he was." Tommy crossed his arms over his chest. Unfortunately, Tommy didn't have the options Ru had. Though he could dance, and his voice was okay, he was not one of the more popular guys of the group and really didn't do well with songwriting. His voice wasn't strong enough to stand on its own, even with a really good songwriter providing music. AJ and Ru had always been the two guys most in the spotlight because of their talent, their looks, and their outgoing personalities. Though Ru was pretty sure that AJ's was 90 percent fake.

In the car on the way back to the condo, Ru was so tired he was dozing, but Tommy was talking. It was pretty late. "I think Katie should book more of those for you. Seems to be a pretty charged crowd. I haven't seen you that connected to your fans in ages."

"Those kids could have been me," Ru told him. "If I wasn't famous. If I had never joined Vocal Growth. You know my dad wanted nothing to do with me when he found out. Mom thinks I'm some sort of devil, and I would be worthless to her if it weren't for the money. After Kris…. Well, I guess I sort of started to believe it too."

"But you're not. You're just you. Ru, the kid with the really amazing voice and this crazy talent for songwriting that can reach the entire world. You just need to get back on your feet. I think the new album is just what you need. Your performances have been great. You were a little rusty in the first show. Don't think I didn't notice you were flat through the first half of 'Fly Home.' But you've still got it. Coming out to the world hasn't changed any of that. Sure, not everyone is going to love you, but how is that different from before?"

Ru shrugged, feeling tears well up, dammit. "I'm just so lonely."

"So find someone. You're a good-looking guy with a lot to offer. Ask someone out."

"And how do I trust anyone again?"

Tommy sighed. "I really wish you'd let me kick Kris' ass."

"Would be really bad media for you."

"But so worth it."

Ru laughed lightly. He pulled his cell out of his pocket to check for a new text. He remembered it buzzing earlier, thinking it was probably a text from the bastard he'd once called boyfriend. He'd been getting texts pretty regularly and ignoring them all. But when the text came up, it was from an unknown number. *Hey, this is Adam, the guy from the library. So you're a Madonna fan?*

OMG!

"What? What is it? What did that bastard do now?" Tommy demanded.

"Not Kris. Adam. The text is from Adam." The time stamp read that he'd actually sent the text a few hours ago. Obviously Ru had been out of range at some point.

"Who's Adam?"

"The guy from the library." Some of the lingering depression began to drop off Ru's shoulders. "He's asking if I'm a Madonna fan."

"Well, there you go. Pretty library boy is gay too. Ask. Him. Out."

"What if he knows who I am?"

"What if?"

"Tommy, I'm serious."

"I am too. You can't hide forever. Famous people find love all the time. Some for a few days, others for years. And if it gets serious, even if he doesn't know you, you'll have to tell him eventually. You've got two songs finished. You just need another eight to make an album. Maybe this guy will inspire you."

"Or break my heart."

Tommy shrugged. "You're only seventeen. If you don't reply, how long will you spend wondering what if?" He shook his head. "No. The Ryunoski Nakimura I know doesn't fear a challenge. He laughs in the face of fear."

Ru sighed and glared at the screen. He quickly programmed Adam's number into his phone, once again wishing he had a picture of the guy. Tommy grabbed the phone from his hands. "Hey!"

Tommy typed out something and hit send. Ru nearly swallowed his tongue.

"What did you send him?"

Tommy threw the phone back, and Ru glared at the screen. *Yes M is my idol. Want to get together some time?*

Ru was going to die. "You're trying to kill me, right?"

"Don't be such a sissy. He'll either say yes or no. Either way, you'll know."

Ru stared at the screen, expecting an answer to come back instantly, but nothing happened.

"It's almost 1:00 a.m., Ru. The guy is probably asleep, like I'd really like to be." Tommy reached over and grabbed his hand to squeeze it. "And no matter what the kid says, you're worth it. You're amazing. And all those kids who meet you at these shows still think you're pretty fucking fantastic."

"You're not going to start reciting the whole 'it gets better' thing, are you?"

"Nope. In time, you'll do one of those on your own," Tommy said as the car stopped. They got out and headed inside. Ru prayed that Adam would return his text, even if it was to just say "thanks but no thanks." Maybe they could be friends. Even that would be better than the loneliness he lived with every day.

CHAPTER 4

ADAM woke up late the next morning, then rushed to shower and to find fairly clean clothes that didn't make him look too prissy, since his parents insisted everything fit well and not be baggy, as was the style in school. His mom appeared downstairs and handed him a breakfast sandwich as he swept up his backpack and practically ran for the door.

"Eat!" she called after him.

"I know, I know. The most important meal of the day," he grumbled at her, then stuffed the sandwich into his mouth before struggling to put on his coat, walk, and carry a book bag all at once. Adam's phone flashed that there was a text he'd missed. He nearly tripped over his own feet and swore his heart skipped a beat. The text was from Ru: *Yes M is my idol. Want to get together some time?*

OMG. Yes, all capital letters. The acronym should have been flashing in giant fluorescent pink letters over his head. There was a second text after the first: *Sorry so late. Was working.*

Both texts had come after 1:00 a.m. Where the hell did the guy work? Maybe he was a college kid after all. But that meant he was out of Adam's league. *Crap.* He should have just called him. Nothing was stopping Adam from doing it now other than his own utter lack of confidence. He wrote back: *NP. Have fb practice after school. Maybe pizza l8r?*

When the reply didn't immediately come, he had to force himself to stop glaring at the screen and get to school. If he didn't get moving, he'd be late, and detention would eat into his practice time.

The phone didn't buzz again until lunch. Bas was sashaying through the lunchroom, while Nate, Jonah, and a bunch of other jocks sat around Adam, pretending they could be gay too. It just made him shake his head at how bad they were when they tried to be the confident guy Bas was. None of them could hold their head that high or smile that broadly and still have it reach their eyes. For all his craziness, Bas knew who he was and was happy being that guy. The jocks were just trying to live up to their fame while they still had it since they had nothing else to offer. Adam wished he could find some of Bas' confidence.

Nate was rambling about how far and at what pace they were going to run tonight, when Adam felt his phone buzz in his pocket and nearly fell over the table pulling the damn thing out. The text was from Ru reading: *Pizza sounds great. Watched u run. :) Can meet u outside school @ 6.*

Adam's heart did that crazy flip-flop thing as he stared at the words and replied back with a simple but stupid: *K.*

Bas plunked down beside him at the jock table, and all the guys started making kissing noises at him. He waved them off. "Pahlease, if you boys knew what was good for you, you'd all be kissing my royal white ass. At least then some of you would graduate on time." He handed Adam a cheat sheet for French. "This is the stuff you were having trouble with. Review it between classes, and you'll be stellar on that test Friday."

"Thanks." The page was pretty short but had some good hints to remember how to say a phrase or remember a response instead of "um, ah, huh?"

"So did you text the sleeping princess your eternal kisses?" Bas asked loudly. So much for it being a secret. Adam was very glad he hadn't shared any details.

Suddenly everyone at the table was looking at Adam with interest. Most of them had girlfriends, cheerleaders, but he thought it was really just for sex, since that's all they talked about. None of them ever seemed to actually go on dates. Maybe that was part of being gay, wanting more; he didn't know, and it worried him a little. "Yeah. We've been texting."

Bas' smile was bright enough to light up the whole lunchroom. Or maybe that was the glitter shadow he wore reflecting in the fluorescents. "Wonderful. See, there is a beginning for everything. Even if you ended up meeting said hottie in a horribly repressive place like the college library." He looked around the table as he said the last word like he was hinting that maybe they should try it sometime. "After all, if a shy cutie like you can meet someone there, maybe the gorillas you sit with could find someone to grunt their intelligible shortcomings to."

"You're just pissed none of us bat for your team, Axelrod," Nate threw back, not letting the ribbing get to him. After all, he was dating the head cheerleader, Lisa Beck, who always wore the shortest skirts and had the biggest boobs on campus. "Must be lonely being the only homo." He fluttered his wrist, which really just looked like he had some sort of muscle spasm.

"Don't, Nate," Adam warned him.

"Dish later, sweetie?" Bas leaned over and kissed Adam on the head, then wandered off. Adam let out a breath he didn't realized he had been holding.

"So you met some hot chick at the library?" Nate asked. "Why did you need to go to the library?"

Adam sighed and for once wished that maybe he was a little more like Bas. Or at least free to just be himself and not worried what the jocks would think about him studying.

Practice went the same as it did every day. The coach paired Nate and Adam, and Nate pressed really hard to keep up. He was getting better, but there was still no chance of him even winning one competition. Yet Nate took more time away from football drills just to run. Adam knew in their region there were four other schools, all with really good track teams. Most of their runners were like Adam, lanky and fast. Just because Northern lacked smaller athletic men didn't mean they didn't have a good sports team. But their basketball and swim teams sucked, and other than Adam, the track team wasn't doing so hot. Football was their only strong point. Maybe Nate hoped it would improve his game in the long run. But Adam thought he played pretty well without having to run. Adam didn't do much in football other than occasionally catch the ball to pass it. He'd been the running back for a while but was tackled so often the coach had benched him. The few times he got to play, Adam often hoped no one would throw the ball his way because even with all the padding, it really hurt to get tackled by guys twice his size.

He spent the two hours trying not to search the stands for Ru. Every time he looked, they were empty. Maybe he wasn't going to come. Maybe he'd only show up after Adam left school. If he wasn't out either, that made sense. Adam still had no idea if Ru was in college or just high school. *Crap.* But at that moment, Adam would have given just about anything to see Ru's pretty pale-blue eyes again.

After he showered, Adam put his school clothes back on and stared at himself in the mirror, suddenly wishing for time to go home and change. Sure, the sweater was okay, fitted and a bright blue, but the jeans were a little snug, too new-looking, and not the distressed wash that everyone wore. His blond hair was too fine to do more than hang in a semilong beach cut. Any time it was shorter, it made him appear almost bald. Adam certainly didn't look like he was ready for a date. But he also knew nothing about what it meant to get ready for a date. *This was a date, wasn't it?*

"Everything okay?" Nate asked as he walked by, filling the doorway like some huge looming shadow. "Are you meeting that girl tonight?"

"No," Adam told him quickly. "Just hanging with a friend."

"Want me to come along?"

"No. I'm good. See you tomorrow. 'Kay?"

"Sure." Nate stepped aside to let him pass, while Adam gathered his bag against his chest like a shield and made his way out. Out of the locker room, out of the school, and finally across the parking lot. A car pulled up beside him as he was wandering around, searching for a glimpse of Ru. The back window went down, and there he was. Dark hair falling around his face, eyes so big and framed by long black lashes, lips just made for kissing….

CHAPTER 5

RU WOKE up at noon that day, somewhat sore and pretty jet-lagged from all the traveling. He'd have to go back to Diego tomorrow to meet with his producer, who wanted to see the songs he'd just finished. But when he woke up to the text from Adam asking for a date, he nearly sprung from the bed with excitement.

He dashed into the living room and across to Tommy's room. Tommy was still asleep, sprawled on the king-sized bed, having fallen there in an exhausted heap after they got home so late. Ru couldn't wait another minute to tell him. So he climbed on the bed and shook his best friend. "Tommy, wake up."

"Is the building on fire?" Tommy asked without opening an eye.

"No, but I will set it on fire if you don't wake up. Adam texted back. He wants to go on a date."

Tommy rolled over and yawned. One eye popped open, and his hair stuck up everywhere, which just made Ru laugh. "Stop laughing at me, you goon. You're interrupting my beauty sleep to tell me you have a date. Awesome. Come back in an hour."

"Beauty sleep?" Ru cracked up even harder, feeling more normal than he had in months. He leapt off the bed and dug through the bedside drawer until he found the huge compact he knew would be in there beside all the condoms and unused breath spray. "Look at how beautiful you are." Ru aimed the mirror at him so when Tommy opened his eyes he was looking right into it.

Tommy nearly fell off the bed. "Damn, you're mean. I told you I need my beauty sleep. See what happens when you interrupt it? I look like a troll."

"Smell like one too."

Tommy flipped him off but crawled up to a sitting position on the bed. "Okay, so talk. Pretty blond boy and date, right?"

"Yeah, we're going for pizza later. I'm going to take him to Dimitri's. I can't believe this is happening."

A grin split across Tommy's face. He reached over and messed with Ru's hair. "See. Just takes time is all. Be patient. Don't push the kid. Maybe this will be good for you. A new start."

"There's only one problem."

"Don't tell me you need new shoes?"

"With your closet across the hall? Not a chance." They wore the same shoe size, so even though Ru couldn't fit into most of Tommy's clothes, he could still borrow a nice pair if he needed to. "I gotta go back to Diego tomorrow to meet with Herb about the two new songs I finished. He's probably going to want to record them right away."

"So you tell your boy that you can hang tonight and will get back together with him when you get back in town."

"He's going to think I'm blowing him off."

"Not if you do it right. And for God's sake, don't screw him or anything on the first date."

Ru frowned at his friend. "Don't be a jerk. You know Kris was the only guy I was ever with."

"I do. I also know that this guy totally turns you on, and you've been without for six months. That's a long time for any guy. I'd be itching for it by now. Just go slow, okay? Starting with sex is never a good way to keep a relationship going." Tommy reached out and hugged Ru. "Now get off my bed. You're almost naked and a guy, so shoo, get some clothes on or something."

Ru jumped off the bed, pulled his boxers halfway up his chest, and walked off like he was some sort of super nerd. Tommy's laughter followed him across the condo. Ru spent the rest of the afternoon going through his clothes trying to decide what to wear. He did end up borrowing shoes from Tommy, but picked a pair of jeans and simple long-sleeved T-shirt for the date.

A dark shirt, Ru decided after staring at his stomach for several minutes. He'd never have flat abs with definition like Tommy or AJ or even Dane. It just wasn't in the cards for him. He could do a million crunches every day and still look like the Pillsbury doughboy. How many magazines had he seen with pictures of him looking huge compared to the other guys, or claiming he'd put on weight?

And then there was AJ. AJ, Mr. Perfect, who made sure he was photographed often wearing little to nothing. Yet the label had lectured Ru about wholesome standards. Didn't matter that AJ, and even Tommy for that matter, had a new girl on their arms for every premiere, every red carpet event or award show. And Dane said inappropriate things all the time to reporters because he just didn't know any better and didn't have a filter for his very chaotic brain.

Ru glared at his reflection, wondering if he should spike his hair and put on some eye makeup. People hit on him in the clubs when he went out that way. Somehow he didn't think Adam would appreciate that side of him so much, the fake spotlight version of him.

"You look good, kid. If your pretty blond boy doesn't like it, then he's not the boy for you." Tommy came into the room and smiled in the mirror at him.

"I want him to like me. Not just how I look or that I sing, or am famous, or have money, but me."

"Well I think you're off to a good start." He held up a piece of paper. "So I looked up your pretty blond boy. Name is Adam Corbin, average student, average kid in general, it looks like. Doesn't have any criminal record or even anything on his school records that says he's any sort of crazy guy or madman looking for fame. Parents are married, registered Democrats, which is the norm in this state. They are Jewish, looks like from his dad's side, and have a medium income for their area. Dad's an accountant. Mom's a buying coordinator for a minor retailer. Adam is an only child, who seems to have only running and football listed as extracurricular activities."

"You researched him?" Ru cried.

"Of course. You didn't think I was just going to let you go out with some guy without looking into him, right? In case you've forgotten, you're famous and people are hella crazy out there." Tommy rubbed Ru's shoulders, trying to ease some of the tension out of them. "And after the crap Kris pulled, well, let's say that no one else is going to get away with that bullshit."

Ru let go of the anger and tried to think it through. Tommy was right. He really should have been more careful. He'd just been so excited that he hadn't thought ahead. Instead of debating on clothes all afternoon, he should have been on the computer and the phone, checking out Adam, ensuring he was safe. Hell, if he'd been smart, he'd have called Katie to do it for him. "Thanks."

"No worries. Now get going. Binks is waiting. Don't want to be late picking up your boy, right?" Tommy held up Ru's wallet. "And try not to go crazy with money stuff. It will be hard enough for this regular kid to take you having a driver. Normal people don't hire drivers."

"Should I drive myself?" The idea had Ru near panicking. Sure he had a license, but he drove almost never and didn't like the idea of driving someplace he was unfamiliar with. "It's so cold out. Are the roads icy?"

"No, you goof. It has to be below thirty degrees to even think about ice. But let Binks drive you. Just don't start buying the guy Rolexes or Mercedes or anything."

"Pizza is okay?"

"You won't have to pay for pizza. Dimitri never charges you."

"I do pay for pizza. I haven't even seen him yet. He's been working. I don't know if he knows I'm in town. It's not like he calls my mom for updates on my status. Last I saw him was for Christmas last year. That was before I was outed to the whole world."

Tommy frowned at him. "Geez, Ru. You have to stop hiding from people. You know big D is not going to have a problem with you being gay. He probably heard it from your mom ages ago. And he's gonna be mad when he finds out you've been here almost a month without seeing him."

Ru shrugged, stuffed his wallet in his pocket, and made his way to the door. "Don't wait up."

"Be back early, Cinderfella. You have to fly to Diego tomorrow and not be a bear when you get there."

Ru saluted him on his way out. All he could think about was seeing Adam again. Talking to him. Maybe getting the chance to kiss him. *Breathe, Ru,* he told himself. *Be the normal confident you. The one you let the cameras see. Not the dependent, unassured guy you hide underneath.*

Binks drove him to the high school, and they circled, watching for Adam to leave the building. Most everyone left from the front of the building because that was the main parking area. Binks must have been privy to Tommy's researched information because he pulled the car up right beside Adam, who was walking along the road. And the guy was just as amazing as Ru remembered. He lowered the window and called out, "Adam?"

CHAPTER 6

"ADAM?" Ru's voice sounded like he'd said it several times before Adam finally heard him.

"Yeah?"

"Are we going to get pizza or no?"

Adam blinked at him for a moment. He glanced at the front of the car, but all the windows were blacked out. Did Ru have a parent driving him? That would be awkward. "Yeah, okay," Adam finally said.

Ru opened the door and slid over. Adam got in and shut the door. The window went up. The back of the car was more like a limo than any normal car he had seen. The seat was wide and had lots of leg room, and the light in the ceiling was on. The seats were leather. He buckled his seatbelt while staring at Ru, who looked amazing in his washed-out blue jeans and snug long-sleeved T-shirt. He was just so beautiful that Adam couldn't do anything but doubt himself in that moment.

"Maybe this wasn't a good idea," Adam told Ru. Was he ready for this yet? He wanted to be, but the queasiness in the pit of his stomach wasn't helping. What if he said or did something stupid?

"Why?" Ru asked. The car was already moving, but there was some sort of divider between them and the driver. All Adam could see was a black wall. "I thought Dimitri's would be good."

Dimitri's was actually the best pizza place in town. The tiny restaurant was known for having private little booths that were clean and well cared for. It was a really popular date place for the college kids. Most high schoolers couldn't afford the steep price of twenty-dollar pies. Adam was more of a five-dollar Hot-and-Ready guy himself.

"How old are you?" He had to ask. Maybe that would be an easy out. There had to be something wrong with this guy that he wanted to hang out with Adam. Maybe he was just older than he looked and really into young guys. That would be sort of creepy, and Adam could escape with an excuse about age pretty easily.

"Seventeen. I'm a Pisces if you're into that sort of thing. How about you?"

"My sign?"

"Well, anything you'd like to tell me would be great. I'd like to know more than just your name, Adam Corbin, and that you like to run."

"You're really only seventeen?"

He nodded. "I feel like eight hundred some days. But yeah, only seventeen."

"I'm a Capricorn, and sixteen," Adam said, not sure what else to say. They sat in awkward silence for a minute. "So, Dimitri's is kind of expensive." Adam had ten dollars in his pocket, more at home if he pulled out his saved allowance. Who usually paid for the date? Did they share? That wouldn't leave enough for drinks and a tip, even if they only ordered one medium pizza, and Adam was crazy hungry.

"Dimitri is a friend of the family, so no worries. I eat there all the time."

"Why me?" Adam blurted out, feeling so out of place in the expensive car with a very handsome guy, who probably shouldn't have even glanced his way twice.

Ru frowned. "What do you mean?"

"I mean, I'm not really the kind of guy…. You're so beautiful. I've never done this before. And me, I'm just—" Adam's words failed as Ru unhooked his seatbelt and slid across the seat. A second later their lips touched, and all Adam could do was hang on for the ride. He closed his eyes and sunk into the soft warmth of Ru's mouth. He tasted like breath mints. For Adam's first kiss ever, it probably ranked on a scale of like 150 out of 10. When Ru didn't pull away right away, but let his lips linger in tiny little kisses, Adam had to open his eyes. Ru's smile was sweet as they stared at each other. Close enough to share breaths and count his eyelashes, which were so long.

"Any more questions?" Ru asked, a light note of humor in his voice.

Adam shook his head, pretty sure he wouldn't be able to form coherent-sounding sentences for the next five minutes or so. And then the car stopped. He glanced up, and sure enough they were at Dimitri's. Ru leaned over and pushed the door open. Adam moved to get out, forgetting he was still buckled for a minute, before struggling out of the car and onto the sidewalk, his cheeks burning with embarrassment.

Ru crawled out after, leaned in as the front passenger-side window went down to say something, then was back in a heartbeat at Adam's side. He slipped his hand into Adam's, and they walked into the restaurant together. His warm grip felt good, right. Some of the tension eased away as a waitress showed them to a booth near the back. Instead of sitting across from Adam, Ru waited for him to slide in and then followed, bumping hips until they could sit together, hands still clasped.

It should have scared Adam to sit that close to Ru. He should have worried that people would see them. But all that mattered was that Ru was there, and he seemed to truly be interested in being with Adam. Adam still really didn't know what to say to him. What did people talk about on dates?

Ru's smile grew a hundred watts, like he could somehow hear Adam's thoughts. "So let's start off with an easy one. What do you like on your pizza?"

Adam glanced away from Ru's face for the first time and then down at the menu he had yet to open. *Crap.* Pizza was kind of messy. Maybe he should have suggested something else. What if he got spices stuck in his teeth or something? "Um...."

"I'm open to anything. You want veggies?"

"No onions," Adam blurted out, thinking of all the date movies he had ever seen. People didn't want to kiss after eating onions, right? Or was that garlic? He wanted Ru to kiss him again. "I sort of like pineapple on my pizza."

"Okay, so peppers and pineapple. You want sausage or pepperoni? Extra cheese?"

"Um, both, I guess? And yeah, extra cheese is good."

The waitress came back, and Ru ordered the pizza, which sounded like it would have to come with a fork and a knife since there was going to be so much on it, and a couple of Cokes. Then the menu was gone and so was Adam's excuse not to look at his date. But he sort of liked holding Ru's hand and sitting there with him. Adam realized just then that he knew nothing about him, not even his last name. And Ru obviously did not go to Adam's school, since he had never seen him around before that day at the library.

"So you don't go to Northern?"

He shook his head. "I'm a homeschool kid. It's awful at times. I mean, my instructor is great, but it's lonely. My only interaction with other kids my age is through message boards, blogs, or e-mails."

"School's pretty bad. The never-ending race to conform." Did he understand that Adam couldn't be out at school? That if people found out, he would get teased and bullied and probably beaten up in the locker room? Bas had been beaten up twice last year, bad enough to be taken to the hospital. Only stricter enforcement of the no-bullying rule at school had stopped that. Adam didn't dare hope it was permanent. Some of the jockstraps had already taken steps to push the boundaries of the no-bully rule. And he remembered what Bas had looked like after the last beating. Dozens of stitches and a face so mottled he had been unrecognizable had made Adam fear standing out. And that was sort of the point. Bullies picked on people not like themselves to make themselves feel better. They didn't like people who shined or did their own thing or just wanted to be individuals. How could Adam tell Ru he was too afraid to be himself?

"I've heard that, but it must be amazing to just be around other people all day. Be able to get into conversations. Ask questions and learn without just reading and writing papers."

"Oh, we still read and write papers. And I'm not so sure the conversations thing is so great. Some of the guys at school can barely follow a 'Good morning.'" Adam thought of some of Nate's friends. He didn't really consider them his friends because they didn't talk, or at least they didn't talk with Adam, usually just at him or through Nate to him. Maybe Adam was as much of an outsider as Bas was sometimes. "I'm not out at school. There is one guy who is, and a lot of the jocks make fun of him. Last year he got beat up a lot. So it's really not all that great to be around a lot of people."

"I get some of that too. But I'm out, pretty much to the whole world. You kiss one boy, someone gets a picture of it on a cell, and suddenly it's front page news." Ru sighed and stared off into space. "But I think it's for the better. It's a lot of work hiding who you are just to please people you really don't care about. The ones who accept you are the only ones who really matter in the end."

He had a point. Adam put his elbow on the table and leaned on his hand to study Ru. "So I'm assuming I'm not your first date."

"No. Sadly. What about you?"

Adam glanced away, not wanting to seem inexperienced and stupid but also not willing to lie. "This is the first time I've been out with anyone, ever." Other than an occasional after-practice meal or an evening studying with Bas, Adam didn't spend time outside of school with anyone.

Ru reached over and touched his chin to get Adam to look at him. God, Ru was so beautiful. "First kiss too?"

Adam nodded, gulping as Ru leaned in again. Adam wanted another kiss so bad it hurt to stay still. "Am I awful?"

"Not at all. It was just the first of many to come," Ru whispered, his lips finding Adam's again. The world ceased to exist when they kissed, time just flying by, people moving around them. Nothing seemed to break the moment, so they were both somewhat startled when someone cleared their throat several minutes later.

The waitress stood there with their pizza. She gave them a sweet smile, set down the pie, and then handed them each plates and silverware. "You two are just so sweet. Let me know if you need anything else."

Once again Adam felt like his face was on fire. He ducked his head against Ru's shoulder as she walked away. Ru kissed Adam's forehead. "Minnesota is surprisingly accepting. Even more so than San Diego sometimes. And like I said, I know Dimitri, so no one is going to be spreading any rumors. Now let's eat, okay?"

Adam nodded and let Ru chose the first piece. Maybe he was just being a kid, but he still didn't want to let go of Ru's hand. Ru didn't seem bothered either, just dished up with his right and helped Adam retrieve a chosen piece. They ate together in a companionable silence. Ru shared his pineapple chunks and Adam his peppers. They snuck kisses in between bites and didn't talk much more until after the last of the pizza had been boxed up.

A large form appearing at their table made Adam shove away from Ru and back into the corner. Ru chuckled. The owner, Dimitri, stood there, arms crossed, looking stern. Adam had met the man before when he'd come in with his parents, but he'd never looked so angry. Then a big smile broke across his face. "Ru! I'm so glad you're back in town. What are you doing here?" He held his arms open.

Ru got up and let the man give him a bone-shattering hug. "Just working on a new project. Wanted some time away from all the lights to get this one done."

"I hear you! When Mona said you were out here, I thought she was pulling my leg. Who's your friend?"

"This is Adam." Adam waved at the big man, heart still pounding but starting to slow down a little. "We met at the library a week ago. What better place to get to have some good food and conversation than here, right?"

Dimitri thumped Ru on the back. "Well then, how about dessert. You like chocolate?" He didn't wait for an answer. "I'll be right back. Go back to cuddling. Don't let me interrupt." He winked at Adam and then headed off to the kitchen.

Ru sat back down and reached for Adam's hand. The younger man let Ru pull him back to his side. "He's sort of a force to be reckoned with."

"I guess."

They both stared at each other, then burst out laughing a minute later. Ru kissed Adam again lightly on the lips while they shared smiles and waited for Dimitri to return. When he did, it was with a huge slice of molten chocolate cake. Adam's mouth watered just looking at it, but Ru looked a little green. Dimitri handed them each a fork. "Dig in, and don't worry about the bill. Everything's on the house."

Adam took a big bite with his fork and shoved it in his mouth. *Oh heaven!* The hot chocolate over the soft and spongy cake tasted amazingly rich. Ru watched but didn't move his fork. "You don't want some?" Adam asked.

"I'm not really a runner like you. And I hate going to the gym." He frowned at the cake. "For each bite of that I take, I'll have to spend another half hour working out."

Adam peered down at Ru's trim body. Sure, he was a little bulkier but not by much. Adam had maybe two inches in height on him, and Ru weighed maybe twenty pounds more. Adam had never really had to worry about his weight, but he knew some of the guys on the football team used protein powder to bulk up, and some of the guys ate a lot of salads to try to slim down. "Okay," he finally said. He took another bite and swallowed, then leaned over to kiss Ru. "But you gotta taste this."

Adam plowed through the cake by himself, letting Ru taste it from his lips. It was romantic, erotic, and peaceful all at once. By the time the plates were cleared away Adam was hoping the night wouldn't end, but they had been there almost two hours. "I feel sort of bad," he told Ru as they walked outside.

"Why?" Ru asked and motioned Adam to walk with him. Since the night was pretty nice, Adam was happy to use it as an excuse to spend more time with Ru.

"I don't even know your last name. We've hardly talked at all. I should know more about you by now. Like your favorite color or maybe what TV shows you like to watch. Or what you wanna do when you graduate." Adam felt a bit like a pervert, clinging to him all night and demanding kisses. But they had been really nice kisses.

"Actually it's kind of refreshing." Ru smiled that radiant smile again. "My last name is Nakimura. Favorite color is red, though it looks horrible on me. I really don't get much time for TV. Sometimes I feel too grown up for my own good, so I think I'll skip that last one. But I do have this thing for cute blond guys who run, and I really like eating pizza with someone I could kiss forever."

They walked about two blocks, hand in hand, before the car pulled up beside them. Adam didn't want the night to end. "Let's go see a movie or something," he blurted out, grasping for anything that would allow them to spend more time together.

Ru stopped and seemed to think it over a minute before finally shrugging and saying, "Sure. But I don't know where a theater is around here. You'll have to give directions."

"No problem. There's one not very far."

They got back in the car, and instead of sitting on the opposite sides of the seat, Adam waited until Ru was buckled and then took the middle seat beside him. Maybe he seemed a little too eager. He didn't care. If the night ended with Ru saying he never wanted to see him again, well, then Adam was going to enjoy every second until that moment came.

They did go to a movie. Adam gave him the directions to a discounted theater he often went to with his parents. The place was fairly well maintained for having such a low ticket cost. The movies were a little older, but that didn't seem to matter. Adam paid for the tickets and led Ru into the big theater. They sat in one of the longer love seats. Having Ru pressed to his side from hip to knee felt pretty good. And Adam was pretty sure their hands would be bonded together permanently by the end of the night. Ru rested his head on Adam's shoulder while they watched, and Adam just breathed in the warm scent of him. He wondered what cologne the man used, or if it was just his shampoo or something as equally unimportant that made him smell so wonderful. When the movie ended, he didn't move. Adam realized after a few moments that Ru had fallen asleep.

"Hey," Adam whispered softly and kissed Ru's hair, which was all he could reach without dislodging the man.

Ru sucked in a deep breath and jolted awake.

"You okay?" Adam asked him. Ru blinked a few times, obviously trying to reorient himself to where they were. The theater lights hadn't come all the way back up, but they were bright enough to show how obviously tired he was. "Let's get you home, okay?"

Adam led him outside, wondering how he would get the car to come back for them. Whoever drove it obviously wasn't family; more of a hired driver, maybe? He had never met anyone with enough money to have a driver, but since Ru didn't seem to be trying to flaunt his wealth, Adam didn't let it bother him.

The car pulled up beside them as though it had been waiting. Adam tapped on the front window to give the driver his address. Once they were inside, the car began to move. It was after ten thirty and curfew was eleven, so Adam needed to be home soon. The text to his mom about hanging with a friend would only get him so far in an argument to avoid being grounded. "Ru, I need to go home."

Ru gripped Adam's hand. "You're going to be mad at me."

Oh no. Here it comes. He was going to say Adam sucked, and he never wanted to see him again.

"I'm going out of town for a few days. I sort of do a lot of traveling between here and San Diego. But as soon as I'm back in town, I'll send you a text, okay? We can go out again? I really want to see you again."

He wanted to go out again? "Sure. I mean it's a family thing, right? Gotta stay with your dad so long and then your mom? I get that. I know some kids who are on a rotation." Though they all went to the same school, and their parents lived just blocks apart.

"Something like that." The car stopped, and when Adam looked up, he realized they were in front of his house. "Text me," Ru said. "Call me. I might not always answer, but I will call back when I have a chance." He leaned forward and kissed Adam so soundly he felt like his toes were on fire. "Promise?"

Adam nodded dumbly and got out of the car. "Thanks, Ru."

His smile was the last thing Adam saw as the car drove away. He tiptoed into the house light as air and dancing on the moonlight. Who knew a trip to the library could put such wonderful things into motion?

His mom and dad only asked him briefly about the night before letting him escape to his room. Once he had closed the door, he leaned against it, looking at where it was he had lived for so long. Everything felt so different, like his senses had finally been awakened. The walls were mostly bare. The only posters were things his mother had insisted on, with quotes about success.

For the most part the room was clean. Adam had a "dirty clothes" pile, a "clean, unfolded clothes" pile, and a "semidirty, he wore it for an hour" pile. His desk was empty of most everything since he hadn't bothered to pull his laptop out of his bag. The only thing that felt real, important, at that very moment was the slip of paper pinned to the otherwise empty corkboard above the desk. It was the paper with Ru's name and number.

Adam sent Ru a quick text thanking him for the evening and telling him how much he would miss him. He had only spent a few hours with Ru, and yet everything had changed. Ru made Adam feel important, like maybe there really was a reason for him to be here. Even if it was just to be crazy about him.

His phone buzzed with a new text: *Can I call u?*

Anytime. Adam wrote back.

A second later it rang.

"Hi."

"Hi," Ru said, sounding tired but happy.

"You get home okay?"

"Yeah. Got an early flight, but I didn't want the night to end yet."

"Me neither." Adam could listen to him talk forever, but nothing was as great as having their hands wound together, or their lips for that matter. "When do you think you'll be back?"

"I don't know. Maybe Sunday. Not sure."

Adam sighed and stripped out of his clothes, threw them into the dirty pile, leaving just his boxers, and got into bed with the phone. Surely it wasn't normal to want someone this much when they had just met?

"You just took off your clothes." Ru sounded like he was smiling huge.

"Are you Superman or something, seeing through walls?"

"No. I heard the clothes rustling. Wish I was there. I bet you've never gotten to hold someone until you've both fallen asleep."

Adam hadn't, and it sounded wonderful. "Someday."

"Yeah." He was quiet for a minute. "What sort of music do you like, Adam?"

"Hmm. I guess I'm kind of eclectic. I like a little of everything. Except rap and country, I think. Madonna's okay, Britney too, but I'm more just whatever's playing. You big into music?"

"Yeah, it's kind of a passion. Grew up with a guitar in my hands."

"Oh no, are you one of those good old country boys?" Adam teased him.

"No way. I'm from Diego, remember? I'm more of a rock guy. Lots of guitars and bass. You ever play anything?"

"Not a drop of musical talent in my body. I was in choir for about five minutes in junior high until the teacher discovered I couldn't find a tune with a GPS. Said something about me sounding like a dying water buffalo."

Ru's laughter was strong and free-sounding, infectious. Adam found himself laughing along with him about his horrible singing skills. They talked a while longer until Adam had a hard time keeping his eyes open. Ru's words merged into a soothing melody that dropped Adam off into a deep sleep without saying good-bye.

CHAPTER 7

TOMMY roused Ru from a dead sleep at three in the morning. "Just kill me now," Ru complained.

"Told you to be home early from your date."

"Eleven is early. Geez." Ru crawled from the bed and into the shower. He must have fallen asleep standing up because Tommy pounding on the door jolted him awake again. "Just a second." Ru scrambled out of the shower and into a clean pair of boxers before opening the door.

"Flight is in an hour. Are you even packed?" Tommy began pulling things out of the drawers: a toothbrush, a hairbrush, the toothpaste. He pointed Ru toward the pile.

"I'm always packed." Ru grabbed the toothbrush and began to foam up. Once he spit out the crap and rinsed, he smiled at his best friend. "Can I tell you about my date?"

"As long as I don't get any erotic details, we're good."

Ru laughed. "We kissed. That's all." And held hands. "He's really sweet. Innocent. I was his first kiss. First date too."

"Wow. Really?"

"Really."

"So he didn't have any boogers hanging from his nose or cigarette breath?"

"Ew. No. Gross."

Tommy grinned. "Awesome. I told you so," he said all singsong like.

"Bastard."

"Uh-huh."

"We ate at Dimitri's. And saw a movie, which I fell asleep in the middle of. Crap. I fell asleep on him." Ru yanked at his hair. At least it wasn't standing up in weird ways like Tommy's was. "I feel stupid."

"You have been traveling for over a week. We both have. I know I'm so jet-lagged my body thinks it's in China right now."

And this trip back to Diego wasn't going to make it any better. "I'm going to be crap to record right now."

"Herb will understand." Tommy stopped shoving things in the small carry-on bag. "AJ, however, won't, if I sound like shit."

Ru sighed. "I wish I could take you with me. Do some sort of duet deal or something. We sound good together."

Tommy shook his head. "I'd just drag you down. You're more rock than I'll ever be. Plus the tabloids are already speculating about my sexuality because I've been at all of your last few shows. They aren't buying that I'm just your BFF, even though that's the truth."

"I'm so sorry!"

"Don't worry about it. I'm a big enough man to not be afraid of it. But we so need to get our asses on the plane." They rushed through the condo, grabbing what they needed in a last-minute rush. Binks was wide awake and chipper when he met them with the car downstairs.

They took a private entrance through the airport, got checked in, and boarded their flight to sit in first class. The flight attendants kept other passengers away as they passed to their seats in economy. Ru put his head on Tommy's shoulder and was asleep before the plane even took off.

His producer, Herb Jensen, sat him down just after noon to discuss the music with him. Herb was probably in his early forties, a tall man with gray hair and a friendly smile. Ru knew Herb was one of the most sought-after producers in the country, which was why he was more than a little nervous to have the man perusing his new songs.

When Herb sat up and looked at Ru, his expression was kind and thoughtful. "You've had a tough couple of months, Ru."

"Yeah, but I think I'm pulling everything back together."

"And these are the first songs you've written since you left Vocal Growth?"

"Yeah." Ru tried to read further into Herb's expression, but the producer must have been used to not showing too much.

Herb pushed the music across the table. "They're okay. Not what I expected from you at this point."

"You don't like them?"

"I think they are just fine if you were a new artist who truly wrote as a seventeen-year-old normally does."

Ru frowned and glared down at the music. He'd been so proud to finally write something. "I don't know what to do. I've had months of nothing. And I worked so hard on these."

"How about a collaboration? We could find some fellow songwriters for you to work with. Or find songs you feel will fit you."

"You mean let someone else write my songs."

Herb nodded. "If you feel like you're truly blocked and that this is the best you can do." He waved to the music in front of them. "They just aren't hit material. And I think you want this first solo album to be big."

Ru looked away, trying to keep the feeling of rejection from overwhelming him. How odd that was. He'd spent years on top, effortlessly, really. What had changed? Why couldn't he connect anymore? Did he really need the other guys of Vocal Growth to be a musician?

"I want you to spend some time in the studio today. Play these songs with the studio musicians. Maybe you'll discover a way to make them better, or perhaps you'll just find that they aren't quite what you wanted to say. Have you been practicing much?"

"Not really." He'd never really had to. Sure, he played his guitar a lot but never had to worry about singing. He'd spent most of his time with Vocal Growth trying to learn the dance moves.

"The voice, and songwriting for that matter, are instruments that need to be played regularly to stay in tune. So I want you to create a schedule. Practice every day, whether it's just to sing 'Happy Birthday' and write a song about spiders. For every ten songs you write, you might have something worth working with. You just need to use your gifts." Herb got up from the table. He paused long enough to pat Ru on the shoulder. "Don't let this break you, Ru. I've watched you grow up in this industry. You have what it takes to become the next legend. I want you to be one of those guys who have fifty years of music topping the charts. You just have to believe in yourself first."

Ru sucked in a deep breath. "Thanks. Okay. Sorry. Thanks." He didn't know what else to say. It hurt to breathe. He wanted to tear up the sheet music as Herb left the room. He fought tears as he grabbed the songs up from the table and made his way into the studio. He wished Tommy was there to help him with the music, or Adam just to smile at him with encouragement. Ru just felt so alone.

When dinnertime rolled around and Ru found himself in the car on the way to his favorite restaurant, he really began to miss Adam. Tommy had to go make peace with AJ, and other than a handful of hangers-on, Ru didn't have much for friends since the picture of him and Kris had been made public. The day had been long and painful. Herb had been right. The songs weren't great. Maybe if he worked on them more, but Ru had that sense of finality that meant the songs were done.

He made his way to a table near the back, where no one would bother him, and brought only his cell and a pad of blank sheet music. He wasn't really hungry, but knew he had to eat, so he ordered a half-dozen entrees to sample and begged the staff to just keep photographers and any other attention seekers away. He had a text waiting for him from Adam. It said, *Running late tonight. Miss u.*

Ru smiled. He could almost see Adam running, his muscles moving like a finely tuned machine. They were so different: Adam into sports and Ru into music. But he couldn't help but hope they would find enough common ground to keep them together for a while. Odd how short a time he'd known the young man, but how much he longed to spend more time with him.

He turned his songbook to a fresh page and began to jot down the lyrics that had been whispering though his head since the moment he met Adam Corbin. A song about beginnings and hopes for something more. It would be a ballad, Ru decided. Maybe even his first single. The words and the music began to pour from him like few songs had before. Maybe Adam would let him sing it for him and not run away screaming from the intensity of the words.

CHAPTER 8

ADAM got ready for school, certain the day would feel endless, but he got up early enough to plug his phone in and actually sit down for breakfast. Even his mom was surprised. She made him eggs, bacon, and a stack of pancakes. He ate, only pausing when he noticed she sat across the table staring at him. "What?"

"Do you have a girlfriend, Adam?" she asked.

Adam swallowed hard. She'd never asked that before. "No."

"Boyfriend?"

How to answer that? He wasn't used to hiding anything from his parents. He'd just never been interested in anyone before. "Maybe?"

"The boy you were out with last night?"

He nodded and just stared at the plate, food in his gut churning. Maybe he should have lied....

"Do you want him to be your boyfriend?"

Adam glanced up and searched her face for any sign of disgust or anger, but found none. "Yes."

She smiled and reached across the table to pat his hand. "As long as he makes you happy." Her eyes scrunched up for a moment. "I wonder if I should have your dad talk to you about the birds and the bees again."

"Oh no, Mom. Really. I know all about that stuff. We had health class, remember?" Even old Mr. Whittleson explaining the needs of personal hygiene hadn't been as embarrassing as Adam's dad trying to tell him about sex.

"Are you planning to have sex with this boy?"

He nearly spit out his orange juice. "Mom!"

"It's a legitimate question. You're sixteen. Boys your age are having sex. Do you need condoms? I should probably research gay sex. Would you need something more than condoms? Do boys use condoms with other boys?"

Adam was pretty sure his face was bright red and couldn't get any darker when his dad walked into the kitchen. Now he was really going to die.

"Did I hear something about condoms?" his dad asked. "Adam, do you and I need to talk about the importance of safe sex again?" *Oh God!*

Adam had never been so grateful to get to school. His parents had been chattering at the kitchen counter about sexual empowerment, gay equality, and how Adam would have condoms available if he needed them. His mom promised to go to the library and look up things about being a gay teenager, and Adam begged her not to. His dad was finally the voice of reason. "He's not ready to be out to his friends, Clara; just give him time. You know how judgmental kids are. How many of your friends told you not to date me just because I was the weird, blond, Jewish boy?"

So just like that, Adam had come out to his parents, and they'd accepted that he was gay. It all felt a little anticlimactic, but he harbored no delusions about it being so easy should he ever decide to let out the secret at school. In fact, that morning he had a creeping sense that someone knew and was just waiting for the right time to break out the news. Maybe it was a lot of teenage paranoia, but Adam kept glancing around searching for someone who might have it in for him.

Nate waited beside Adam's locker near the end of the day. Bas stood there too, looking pissed. "Everything okay, guys?" Adam had to ask as he stored away his algebra book, really hoping this wasn't some sort of intervention/welcome to the club deal.

"Nate thinks you should skip study hall to go run. I told him you'll be running after study hall anyway, so why skip it?" Bas told Adam.

"I was just saying that it couldn't hurt to get more practice. We have a bunch of games coming up," Nate pointed out.

"Okay, but I have a French midterm on Friday, and I really need to study. So no skipping study hour, but I can stay late if you want to keep going after practice." It's not like Adam had anywhere to be, anyway, since Ru wasn't in town. His only text had been a brief *I miss u* and that had been after lunch.

Nate frowned but finally shrugged. "Fine. See you at practice, Corbin." He wandered off down the hall in the direction of the gym.

"That guy is a total meathead," Bas grumbled. "And he wants in your pants, in case you can't tell. A gay man knows these things."

"Bas, Nate is just pushing himself really hard for that scholarship."

"Uh-huh."

Adam held out his French book to him. "So are we going to study, or are we going to discuss the boring jocks of this school?"

Bas took Adam's arm and led him to the computer lab, not study hall. "You are going to sit down and take a test."

"Huh? Like a trial French exam or what?"

"No, an interests calculator. It's something that is supposed to help you decide what you want to do with the rest of your life. You are severely lacking focus." He leaned over and keyed in a web address. "Just answer the questions as honestly as you can, easy peasy."

"What about the French midterm?"

"You're doing better in French 3 than most of the kids in AP."

Adam blinked at the screen and the looming questions. What exactly did this test tell anyone? Would he come to the end and it would scream gay, clueless, and sixteen? The first question was a group of five multiple choice from Never to Always, beginning with: You like creative ideas.

Okay, he could do this. Adam clicked through the questions, not spending much time lingering over each one and just going with his initial reaction. When he reached the end and clicked submit, the page flipped and Bas reappeared. According to the survey, Adam was a visionary. And the list of careers? He sighed. "I'm still wishy-washy," he told Bas.

"Not at all. You're just a helper, is all. You just need someone or something to take care of. You have creativity that needs to be tapped and focused into a project." He plunked down in the chair next to Adam and opened a notebook. "So what subjects do you actually like?"

Adam smiled. "Track."

Bas sighed and let his head thump on the table.

After Adam answered a heap of questions, Bas told Adam he would do some research and get back to him. The only thing they'd discovered was that Adam sort of picked things up without really trying to learn them when it came to math and science, but also had a way with writing that made Bas think Adam was meant to be some sort of Pulitzer Prize winner. Adam's reading comprehension was good, but his attention span was questionable if doing anything other than running.

Adam had hundreds of notebooks full of random ramblings, incoherent thoughts he just poured out to pages to clear his head when running wasn't enough. Once he'd learned to type in the sixth grade, he'd transferred most of it to his computer in neat little files labeled by years and topics. He was pretty sure no one was going to look back at all that and think he was changing the world.

By the time study hall was over, Adam was happy to get away and even happier to get the chance to put on his running shoes and just let go. No other texts had arrived from Ru, and yesterday sort of felt like a sweet dream that was slowly fading. Once Adam began to run, he just let it all go and let his body work.

Nate kept up better than he had been. When the whistle blew as a reminder for them to speed up after the tenth lap, Adam really set in for the long haul and stopped caring whether or not anyone could keep up.

Since it was now a week into October, the air had begun to take on a deeper chill. Snow began to fall, and his lungs really burned but in a good way. He didn't realize until the final call that he'd left everyone behind and done nearly twice the laps. Even Nate had fallen back, panting and clutching his side. Everyone else was off doing other drills.

Adam slowed as he approached Nate. "Do you still want to stay late?" Adam asked through heavy breaths. His body was warm, fluid, and he could probably go for another hour or two.

Nate shook his head. "I thought I was catching up. Thought maybe I had a chance, but wow. You just flew by me like you had fucking wings, Corbin. I'm an elephant compared to you. And Northern doesn't have a chance as a track team, but you sure as hell have a chance to get to state without us."

Adam frowned at him, wondering if he was saying what he was hearing. "We need at least three to compete. Six for a chance at nationals, and it's more than six months until the first competition. You're giving up?"

"I'm never going to be as fast as you."

"You don't have to be as fast as me. You just have to be faster than the other guys." They stared at each other for a few minutes. Nate finally looked away. "You want to give up, then fine. You can spend more time practicing tackles, not a big deal. I'd rather run than get thrown to the ground by a couple of three-hundred-pound gorillas." He glanced at the jockstraps, who were lingering near the course, and realized just how true those words were. Maybe it was time for him to give up the ghost and let football go.

Nate flinched. "Yeah, about that. I know they've been bugging you."

"Not any more than normal." The jockstraps always had it out for anyone who wasn't like them: huge, dumb, and slow. Adam was fast enough and smart enough to stay out of their way.

Nate shrugged and held out his hand. "Still friends?"

Were they? Adam had never really thought of Nate as one, but he took his hand anyway. "Yeah. You ever want to run, let me know." Adam let him go and headed over to the coach, who was packing up his gear.

Once Adam actually got home and sat down, the activities of the day really started to wear him down. The phone ringing yanked him out of a light sleep. It was just after nine, and Adam was still fully clothed lying in bed. He kicked off his shoes and reached for his cell. The name on the screen brought a smile to his face. "Hey."

"Hey," Ru said. "How was your day?"

"I missed you, but I ran like a frickin' demon."

"Yeah?"

"It was like flying."

"So why do you sound sad?"

'Cause you're not here, Adam thought. "No one else wants to run. I talked to the coach. He encouraged me to stay on the football team but says there probably won't be enough guys signing up in the spring for a whole track team. Means I go back to mostly warming the bench for football."

"That sucks. You're not going to stop running, though, right?"

Adam thought about it for a minute and realized that for all his undecided wishy-washiness, running was something he did really like. Too bad there wasn't anything he could do with it long term. "I guess I could get up early and run."

"You could train for a marathon. Get sponsors, pick a cause. It would give you a reason. Something to motivate you."

"Yeah, that's a good idea." Adam wished Ru were there so he could kiss him and stare into those pretty blue eyes. "How was your day?"

Ru laughed lightly, but it was strained. "Okay. Busy mostly. Did some work, studied a little, took a nap since I'm off on time zones again. My boss gave me a bit of tough love, so that was hard."

"Aw."

"I miss you."

"Yeah?" Adam asked and got up from the bed to begin very nosily taking off his clothes. Ru sucked in a deep breath. "You hear that?"

"That was your shirt."

"Mhmm. And this?" Adam unzipped his pants.

"Christ."

"Nah ah. I'm Jewish. Try again."

Ru's laugh was more real this time as Adam slid his pants off. "You're incredible."

"'Cause I strip over the phone for you? I don't think you'd be as impressed to see it in person. I'm not much of a dancer, though I do the white-boy wiggle." Adam shook his hips around to an imagined generic beat. "You'd so be laughing your butt off right now."

"I don't know how it's possible to be this crazy about you, Adam. Do you get that? I've known you for less than a week, and I'm obsessed with you. I want to know everything about you. Want to sleep in your bed wrapped around you, watch you do your cute little dance, and kiss your amazing lips until the world stops moving. That is not normal."

"Hmm. You say all that like it's a bad thing. But I sort of like it. Well, not sorta. I really do like when you say nice things to me. No one has ever even looked at me before. And you're so beautiful. I just keep thinking you're going to wake up soon and realize you can do so much better than the blond Jewish boy from Minnesota."

"I'll be in late Saturday night. Will you wait up for me?"

"I can get one of my folks to pick you up at the airport."

"I have a driver for that. It's you I want to see. Will your parents get mad if I come by late?"

After the discussion this morning, Adam was pretty sure they were just going to embarrass him. "They offered to buy me condoms. And my mom is researching gay sex, probably as we speak."

"You told them?"

"That I'm gay, yeah. It just sort of came out this morning at breakfast. My mom was asking if I had a girlfriend and I said no, and then if I had a boyfriend and I said maybe. I mean, are you and me…? I mean…." Was it too much to ask for so soon?

"I'd like that."

"Being my boyfriend, you mean?"

"Yes."

His whole world snapped together in a moment of instant harmony. Ru liked him, he really liked him. Adam was suddenly giddy enough to jump up and clap as he did another little hip jiggle. "Woo-hoo." He swayed around the room like a maniac.

"I need to see this dance of yours."

"Saturday night. I'm so happy right now."

Ru laughed. "'Cause I said I'd be your boyfriend?"

"Yes."

"I don't know how I've made it this long without knowing you."

"Ru—"

"Seriously. Sometimes I'm just so lonely and everything is so overwhelming. Now I have something to look forward to. Your texts are like a lifeline."

"I'll send more, then."

"But they're not as good as being with you in person. We need to go out again."

"We could do pizza at Dimitri's again. Dimitri seemed really nice."

Ru let out a sweet sigh. "We can go there every night if you want. I will do a lot just to kiss you again and to hold your hand."

And just like that, Adam wished he was there, could almost imagine Ru leaning in to kiss him again. "It's only Wednesday. And I have a French midterm Friday."

"*Meilleurs voeux, mon ange*," Ru said with a perfect accent.

"I didn't know you spoke French."

"Been to France a time or two."

"You know you are so out of my league we aren't even on the same planet, right?"

"Why would you say that?"

Because he obviously had money coming out of his ears. He spoke French like he was born there and looked like he could be the baby of some of People's Most Beautiful winners. "You're perfect and beautiful."

"Not perfect. The other stuff is subjective. You, however, are amazing. I wish it were Saturday. I'm sorry about your track team."

"It's okay. I don't need other people with me to run. It's sort of a solitary sport."

"Yeah, I thought that way about myself for a while. But I don't want to be a solitary sport, Adam. I want to be with you."

Adam couldn't keep the smile off his face. "So when you're here where do you stay? Like with a parent?"

"My folks aren't really involved in my life. I think my mom is on a cruise somewhere in Europe with boyfriend number who-knows, and I haven't seen my dad since I was eleven. There's this really nice condo in downtown that I'm borrowing from a friend."

"And you stay there all by yourself?" Adam didn't care much for downtown, though he had been told it had a lot of great clubs and restaurants. It was almost an hour drive to get there, and the parking was more than a week's allowance. Unless he was going to a game, it was unlikely he would venture that far from home. "So you have to cook for yourself? My mom and dad wanted me to cook once a week, but after three consecutive weeks of trying and serving up burned, barely recognizable food, they put an end to that. Which was good. I like the idea of cooking, but the directions are always so long, and I'd rather be running."

Ru laughed. "I can cook. Sometimes I hire a cook if I know I'm going to be busy. But I do okay. I'll cook for you sometime."

"Okay. I'd like that. But it makes me sad that you go to this condo and are all alone."

"It *is* lonely sometimes."

"I can imagine."

Ru sighed deeply. "I better go. I'll try to call you again. But if things get too crazy, don't think it's 'cause I'm ignoring you. I'm not. I promise."

"Okay. I'll miss you."

"And you have no idea how happy that makes me." They ended the call with that.

CHAPTER 9

Ru HUNG up the phone feeling lighter. He picked up his guitar and leaned back against a stack of pillows. His apartment in San Diego was nowhere near as grand as the place Tommy had in Minnesota. He could have afforded something bigger with an indoor pool and his own studio, but he liked the open space and industrial walls of his loft. He didn't need something that designers created to make his life a showcase. He just needed comfort, which was why the furniture was more for comfort than style, and the square footage was more of what an average person would have rather than that of someone with millions of dollars to spend.

He could play as loud as he wanted and not bother anyone else in the building, and though he knew there were other musicians in the place, he never heard them. All he could think about tonight was Adam, his little phone striptease, and how much hearing his voice had changed the course of his day.

Ru strummed out a few chords, ran through a couple of Vocal Growth songs before moving on to practice some of his favorite musicians' work. Most of the stuff he was playing should have been performed on one of the five different electric guitars hanging on his wall, but he really liked the acoustic. It felt good in his hands and sang sweetly to him. When he finally turned to the song he'd been working on for the past few hours, the melody just flowed.

He let his voice free, not worrying about matching up to anyone else or balancing out someone's bass; it was all him. He sang the song as though he were singing it to Adam, smiling when the song turned suggestive and softening his tone when it turned sweet. After a few adjustments, Ru finally put the guitar aside.

His phone buzzed. A text from Tommy. *How was your day?*

Long, Ru texted back. *Herb didn't like songs. Starting over. U?*

AJ is douche.

LOL, Ru replied. *Really, is everything going to be okay?*

Probably. New guy is like AJ junior. Miss you already. So, bad songs?

Working on a new one now.

Yeah?

Cheesy love song.

LOL. About Adam?

Maybe, Ru wrote back. *Definitely.* He wanted to go back to Minnesota so bad, and not for the weather.

Come to studio. We'll work on song together.

What about AJ?

Left an hour ago. Just me. AJ says my voice blows.

Ru groaned but got up to pack up his guitar. As much as he didn't want to go out, he would. He would do just about anything to improve his music, and maybe Tommy could help. *Be there soon.*

At the studio a little while later, almost everything was dark, but the security guard let him in. Ru found Tommy in the band room plunking around on the keyboard. He'd forgotten the guy grew up playing the piano. Tommy looked up and smiled. "So where's the song? Let's hear it."

Ru cringed. "I don't know."

Tommy glared at him. "Seriously, man. It's me. Sit the fuck down and sing it. If it sucks, I'll tell you so, and then we can fix it."

"You didn't tell me the other ones sucked."

"'Cause they don't. They just aren't great."

Ru growled at him. "You could have said something before I showed them to Herb and made a fool of myself." He pulled the music out of his folder and went to the copier to get an extra for Tommy to read.

"Herb is your producer, and it's his job to produce good results from you. My job is to be your friend and supportive no matter what. Besides, they were pretty good for a guy who hasn't written anything in months." Tommy took the music and sat down at the keyboard. He read it over for a minute before grabbing a pen and jotting down a few things.

"Changing it already?" Ru asked in dismay.

"Just adding some piano, kiddo. This is a Ballad with a capital B. Needs the keyboard. Sit down, play, sing. Don't mind me."

Ru sat down on the wooden stool and adjusted the mic before pulling up his guitar. The song began slow, a tentative touch, like that first kiss, and talked about how meeting someone could blow apart the whole world. He sang about the scars of his past being put to rest, then began the chorus, which Tommy joined in without prompting with a soft harmony to Ru's powerful tenor melody. Then on to the second stanza about wanting to find out what would happen next in their relationship. By the time Ru got to the bridge, he had tears streaming down his cheeks and was singing like he hadn't in years. Maybe the practicing really was helping. He'd been singing for hours already before meeting up with Tommy.

When the last strum of the guitar had faded, Tommy left the keyboard, crossed the room, and wrapped his arms around Ru. "You are crazy in love with this boy already, and you barely even know him."

Ru didn't know what to say. He felt like the song had torn all the words from him and set them free. Yeah, he was crazy about Adam Corbin. He hoped beyond all hope that what they had was the stuff of legends but knew it was far too soon to speak of it.

"And that song, kiddo, was phenomenal. Just a few nitpicks, and then we can play this for Herb tomorrow," Tommy said as he returned to the keyboard and the notes he'd made.

"I don't think I can do this without you, Tommy. Do you know how amazing we sound together?" Ru turned to his best friend.

"Yep. That's why I'm gonna sing back up for your album. No need to ask." His grin was huge. "And AJ is gonna be so pissed when this song is number one, and his doesn't even hit the top ten."

"He's written a song?"

"A ballad. One where Dane, Newguy, and I stand in back swaying and doo-wopping. I don't doo-wop."

Ru just shook his head, unable to believe the nerve of AJ. Vocal Growth had made millions off their harmonies. Sure, they all had occasional solos, but that would be one part of a song, not a whole song, and they had never just been background noise. "Okay, nitpick away. Let's get this hammered out. Maybe I can sing it to Adam."

"Have you told him yet?" Tommy asked, suddenly very serious.

"Told him what?"

"Who you are."

Ru frowned at his music stand.

"You have to tell him, Ru. What if he finds out some other way? He'll be pissed you've been hiding it from him."

"I'll tell him soon. Honest. I just sort of have to figure out who I am first." Ru picked up his guitar and began to strum. Maybe he was finding his way.

CHAPTER 10

ADAM spent most of the next few days thinking about Ru and sent him a few texts but got no reply. Without track or Ru, Adam really didn't know what to do with himself. In class the teachers never called on him, though he almost always knew the answer. Ru said he never got to experience a classroom. When he asked questions, it was via e-mail or a text message. He never got face-to-face interactions. That bothered Adam a lot, especially since Ru seemed to be a very extroverted guy. He spoke with his body through gestures and facial expressions that Adam had only had a single date to memorize. Maybe soon they would have more time together so he could learn more about the mechanics that made up Ru Nakimura.

Over that Thursday and Friday, Adam did something unthinkable: he raised his hand to ask and answer questions. Sometimes even a heated discussion would come up, and normally he would back away, but now he was getting involved, wanting to interact if only to be able to tell Ru about it later. When it came to his French exam, Adam flew through the written portion and when Mademoiselle Rochelle sat him down for the oral, he wasn't even nervous. He talked about sports he liked and what he thought he would do over the holiday break that would come in a few weeks, but he didn't once stumble or find himself lost for words. He owed Bas a huge thank-you for all his help.

Adam kept notes of all the interactions and his feelings about them. He added pages and pages of content to his ramblings and saved them to his computer. So much was devoted to Ru and Adam's attempt to live actively for him that he ended up texting the man for his e-mail and then sending him the folder unedited. Adam worried only a little. He figured Ru would probably glance at the ramblings and move on. He just wanted Ru to know what it felt like to be in school—the good, the bad, and the horrible.

After French class, Adam was on his way to study hall when he was stopped by Nate's jockstrap friends. "Yo, Corbin, you should stop hanging so hard on Nate. He's not like you and your fairy friend Sebastian."

Adam blinked a few times, trying to sort through the words, all while fear crept into his brain. *Did they know? And how could they?* "I don't know what you're talking about. Nate just wanted help with his running. He's trying for a scholarship from the U of M."

The guy known as Hank the Tank shoved Adam into the wall of lockers. "He's not a braincase like you."

"Obviously," Adam snarked back, rolling his eyes. He wasn't going to let these oversized morons bully him. Once they thought you were weak, they attacked in hordes. "Or he wouldn't have to try to get a scholarship with his poor track skills. And if Nate can't get one, the rest of you are sure up a creek sans paddle."

Hank made a move to hit him, but Nate appeared and grabbed his hand. "What the hell, man?"

"Just warning your *friend* to keep his distance." The two squared off like they were going to fight.

"Seriously," Adam said. "Are you really that stupid? It's the middle of the school day. You'll be suspended for fighting. Homecoming is in few weeks. Suspension means neither of you will be playing for homecoming. Think about it, Hank." He turned and walked away from them all, holding his head up, though he was quaking down to his toenails. He'd just faced down Hank the Tank. Almost got beat too. As Adam headed to study hall, praying no one would follow him, he dug through his backpack for his laptop and planned to use the free time to write about bullying at Northern High.

He remembered back to when Bas had first been attacked. It had been after Homecoming last year. Adam found him in the boys' bathroom in one of the stalls. He remembered standing there for a minute or so, just blinking at the sight. Now thinking back on it, it looked as though Bas had not only been beaten; something more had happened. The images wouldn't come together in Adam's mind: blood, the bruises, the memory of Bas' mostly nude body. Adding that into the context of Northern High's bullying made his heart leap in fear. Bas never talked about it, but he also avoided the bathrooms and the locker room like they were Nazgûl death camps.

Adam thought hard about the things Bas did and wondered just what it was that offended people. He wore makeup, but not as much as most of the girls, and his was usually better applied. He had a pretty good sense of style, wearing things mostly only seen in magazines, and he was super smart. Bas would likely graduate valedictorian. He probably had a scholarship lined up for some Ivy League school. And Adam suddenly felt bad because he didn't really spend much time with Bas and had never done anything to seek him out for fear of what others would say. In not standing up for one of the only guys he considered a friend, he was essentially saying it was okay for everyone else to bully, not only Bas, but anyone. Adam sighed and glared at his computer screen.

He did a search online and discovered his mother had bookmarked some things for him, including the Rainbow Dash, which was a run at the Pride fest in downtown Minneapolis next June. The Pride was also looking for volunteers, and the Dash would require him to find sponsors. He'd have to come out to do those things. But maybe, now that he wasn't alone since he had Ru, he could find the strength to stand out just a little.

When class ended that Friday, he had an idea, and instead of going to practice, which was now all tackling and throwing since no one wanted to run anymore, Adam sent Nate a text that he had something to do and headed home instead. No need to give the jockstraps another opportunity to beat on him. His mom was making dinner when he arrived.

"You're not running tonight, Adam?" she asked.

"I don't know if I want to play football anymore." His shoulder ached from being jarred by Hank last night and again today with the shove into the lockers. Why was Adam trying to be something he wasn't? He hated football. Watching it, doing it, and a lot of the guys playing it. Sure, he wasn't going to go and join the drama club, but maybe he could focus on something else. He knew the school newspaper was always looking for people to join. He liked to write. Maybe he'd do that and just avoid reporting on sports. Not that he planned to give up running. "Ru suggested I train for a marathon or something. Raise money for a cause. I saw the bookmark you left me for the Rainbow Dash."

"That's a good idea. I bet your dad would run with you." She was making eggplant lasagna, Adam's favorite. Instead of noodles, the eggplant would be sliced thin and layered between the cheese, sauce, and meat. "You're not going out with Ru tonight?"

"He's in San Diego until tomorrow night." Adam tapped his fingers on the table, wondering what she would say. "I was wondering if maybe he could come stay with us. You know, like just for the weekend or something. He doesn't really have anyone. His mom is off in Europe somewhere, and it sounds like his dad and him don't get along...."

"Where does he stay when he's here?"

"Some condo downtown."

"I'll talk to your father about it. You know he'll have to stay in the spare room."

"Contrary to what you and dad think, I'm not a horndog. We just kiss and hold hands, is all." Still Adam felt like his cheeks were burning just from admitting they touched at all. Maybe he was just a little slower to mature than some of the other kids, but he couldn't imagine that having sex would uncomplicate their relationship at all. And he didn't feel emotionally ready for that yet anyway. He heard about other guys jacking off to pictures and keeping a stash of nude magazines under their bed. Adam hadn't ever found the need to touch himself that way, and his stash of magazines was on a shelf for all to see. But somehow he figured he got more out of *The Running Life* than the other guys did from their porn.

His mom leaned over and kissed his head. "I'll talk it over with your dad. If you're going to run at all tonight, you best go now. The forecast is predicting snow."

The clouds did look heavy and gray. Adam went up to his room to change, put on a better pair of running shoes and the waterproof pants, and headed out to the trail that passed behind his suburban home. Most of the trail was pretty empty this late in the year, bikers and skaters frightened away by the damp cold. Adam just got lost in the rhythm of his feet. His phone buzzed sometime later, and for a moment he thought it was Ru, but it was just his mom telling him dinner was almost ready. Adam had been moving for an hour and a half. The snow was really coming down. If he went to the streets and cut through some blocks, he could probably make it back home in thirty minutes or so.

He cut through a neighbor's yard and headed for the road. He was almost hit by cars three times as they slid, swerved, and drove wildly in the snow. Finally he'd taken to the unplowed sidewalks, slogging through a half foot of snow, pants and shoes soaked. So much for waterproof. Adam couldn't run anymore because the ground had started to freeze and was now one endless ice rink. If winter was starting bad this soon, it was going to be a hell of a long haul.

An SUV pulled up beside him, and he had to glance twice before he realized it was his dad. "Your mom was getting worried. It's pretty awful out here."

Adam hopped in, and his dad plopped a fleece blanket into his lap. "Let's get you home and warmed up. Food should be ready."

He drove, and they said nothing for a few minutes. Adam blinked through his soaked hair, which was hanging in his eyes, but the warmth blasting from the heaters had begun to thaw him out. It made him think more about Ru, and how he didn't seem to have anyone that cared. Would anyone have picked Ru up in the storm, remembered to bring him a blanket, or even cared that he hadn't made it home for dinner?

"Thanks, Dad."

His dad glanced Adam's way and threw him a sunny smile. The blond hair came from him, and everyone always remarked at how young he looked. Too young to be the dad of a teenager like Adam. And then they'd go on to ask why he'd only had one child. Truth was, Adam's mom almost died having him. Something about her hips being too small to bear children easily. She'd been on bed rest for months. And 'cause his dad loved her, he wasn't going to risk her again. "For what?"

"For being okay with me being me."

He reached out and messed up Adam's hair. "Baby boy, you are exactly as you are supposed to be. Don't let anyone else tell you otherwise."

A lot of people grumbled about their parents, and Adam got it, he really did. Sometimes they were pretty uncool, like the whole condom thing. But the truth was his parents cared about him. They watched his grades, went to all his conferences and track meets. They monitored what TV shows he liked, books he read, and what he saw on the Internet. They never outright reprimanded him for those choices, just made gentle hints about what they would prefer for him.

He was probably the only kid at Northern High without a Facebook page. That used to bug him, but now with all the peer pressure and bullying, he didn't really mind it. No matter what happened during the day at school, he went home, and it all ended. What he didn't know couldn't hurt him, right?

They pulled into the driveway, but before Adam could get out, his dad grabbed his arm. "Your mom told me that you want this boy to come stay with us. I don't think that's a good idea."

Adam began to protest, but his dad shook his head.

"Hear me out. You haven't known him that long, right?"

Adam nodded.

"He has a roof over his head and food, right?"

Again he nodded. "He goes back and forth to San Diego all the time, and no one seems to care about him. No one wants to take care of him. But I do. I want to show him what it's like to have a family and maybe not have to sit alone in some fancy condo."

"I understand that this is important to you. I also know that this is new to you."

"Very important. He's important."

His dad nodded. "He can stay Saturday night and through the day on Sunday, then he has to go home. And you'll both stay in separate rooms. We'll try it once."

"Dad, I'm not ready for sex yet. Even if he did stay in my room—"

"Which he won't be. Adam, you are very young. I understand more than you know how much you want this to work. First loves, well they are sort of like rainbows and sunshine all swirled into one. I want this to be good for you. I want him to be good for you. But teenage boys have hormones, and sometimes they get out of control. I don't want you looking back and regretting this."

Adam stared out the window feeling like he wanted to cry. It sounded to him like his dad thought this was just a short-term thing. He hadn't even met Ru yet and probably thought him out of Adam's league.

His dad sighed heavily. "I want you to be happy. I do. Can we just do this a little slower? Your mom and I need to adjust too. We want to help you work this stuff out, but you have to let us." His dad squeezed Adam's hand. "Saturday night and Sunday during the day. And if he's under our roof, he'll have to follow our rules. That means for the Internet too. I know everyone's got iPads nowadays...." And just like that he was off on some ramble about the evils of the Internet. Adam got out of the car and headed toward the house. He and Ru would have a day and a half together. That had to be better than Ru going off to some lonely high-rise. Adam headed to the shower, breathing in the sweet smell of dinner as he went. How many homemade dinners did Ru get?

CHAPTER 11

HERB loved the song and insisted Ru record it right away, then spent the next few days editing and hyping it to some of his local radio buddies, which got Ru an invite to perform on a late-night show. So instead of getting ready to fly back to see Adam early, Ru was in hair and makeup in LA on some studio set, with Tommy perched over on the sofa watching. They had made it official, announcing that Tommy was doing backup vocals on Ru's new album, which sent the media into another frenzy.

"Afterward we have a party to meet some radio guys," Tommy was saying.

"I just want to go back to Minnesota." He wanted to see Adam. He hadn't had time to do more than text him a handful of times in the past few days.

"You will. Your flight doesn't leave till late tomorrow."

"How'd you convince AJ to let you be here, anyway?" Ru asked.

"I told him that if he started spewing hate, I'd reveal his concert secrets."

Ru turned to look at his friend despite the protests of Lily, who was working on spiking his unruly hair. "You are going to make him hate you."

"He already hates me. AJ hates anyone who isn't AJ. Did you see that picture he posed for in *Teen Celebs*? I was like, dude, you're not even a teen, you poser, and talking about how being inspirational for fellow teens is so important. That guy sends my bullshit meter off the chart." Tommy tied his shoes and stood up, looking more like a European glam star than the American boy-band prince he was.

Lily giggled.

"What? It's true?" Tommy protested.

"I know," she said. "I've done his hair." And just like that she went back to fitting Ru into the rock-star image he'd created for himself since leaving the group, which included lots of eye makeup, high hair, and even glittered platform heels he'd had to special order.

When all the primping was finished, Tommy and Ru were herded out of the dressing room for pictures. After a million poses and flashes, they were finally allowed to head to the stage. Tommy patted Ru's back and whispered, "Good luck."

Ru had to talk first then he'd get to perform. When he'd been part of Vocal Growth, AJ had done that part. Now it was all on him. He put on his game face and made his way out into the crowd, waving, shaking hands, smiling. Everything felt surreal, but when he shook the hand of the host, who he couldn't remember the name of, and sat down, he just gave it his all.

The questions were as easy as Katie, his manager, had promised they would be, even when asked about his homosexuality. Ru was prepared. He'd spent a few hours reading Adam's rambling. Knew about the bullying at school—from Adam's out friend Bas who'd been beaten up bad enough last year to require a couple dozen stitches, to Adam's encounter with a football teammate.

Ru spoke about the importance of young people having support, about how difficult it was to come out in a world where being gay was scorned, and how bullying had to be stopped. He talked about statistics and his work with LGBT shelters and the Trevor Project. He didn't know how much of it would actually make it to the air, but he felt good when he finally got up and went to the mic.

Once he'd picked up his guitar, he was back in his element. He looked into the camera, knowing Tommy was on the board behind him, though he could have asked for any studio keyboardist in the country. When Ru began to play, it was for Adam, the sweet song of new beginnings. The audience was on their feet, moving and cheering before he was halfway through the number, and when he let his voice take over for the bridge, showing them his true skill and range, the cheering was deafening. All in all, an amazing performance.

Ru had been practicing all day long, every day, since his talk with Herb. The producer had been right, of course. His voice was an instrument and his songwriting a talent, both of which needed practice and fine-tuning. He'd rewritten his two other songs; one was based almost completely on the story Adam told in his journals about Sebastian. That song he had already recorded and donated to LGBT youth shelters, the song and all proceeds from it.

The lights faded, and Ru felt Tommy grab his hand as they were led off stage. Once away from the crowd, Tommy threw his arms around Ru and hugged him hard. "You were so incredible."

Ru blushed. "I was just being me." The fashionable chunk of hair left free to hang down bugged him when he glanced up. "With more makeup and hair gel than most of the western world, but still me."

Tommy laughed and put his arm around Ru's shoulders, walking them toward the dressing rooms. "See, and you were all worried. I bet that performance will be on YouTube in an hour. You should send it to Adam."

"Not yet," Ru said. He wasn't sure how he'd tell the young man about his horribly repressive fame. The fact that announcing anything about their relationship to the media might just kill it before it began had crossed Ru's mind a time or two. He didn't want to drag Adam into the spotlight. That had to be Adam's choice, and if they stayed together it would happen eventually.

A photographer snapped a photo. Ru frowned. There weren't supposed to be more photos after the show. That's why they'd taken them before.

"Tommy, are you and Ryunoski an item? Is that why you're here with him and not in San Diego with Vocal Growth?" the photographer asked.

"I'm here supporting my best friend," Tommy said. He dropped his arm. "Security!"

The camera kept flashing. Ru felt blinded for a minute but let Tommy and then Security lead them away to a secure area of the building. Tommy's phone rang, and he went to take the call, leaving Ru alone in his dressing room. Ru stared at himself in the mirror, a little shocked by what he saw. Was that really him? He looked beautiful, like some work of art, flawless skin and smoky eyes. But it didn't feel like him. This persona seemed more like a mask to hide what he didn't want to show the world.

Tommy returned. "Let's get to the party." He paused when he saw Ru staring in the mirror. "Did you want to change?"

Ru shook his head. "This is who I have to be, right? For the cameras?"

"You can be whoever you want to be, Ru."

"But I'm gay. So this is what they expect of me. Some glammed-up queen."

"Not feeling pretty?" Tommy's tone was light and teasing.

"I'm beautiful, but you know I'm not really."

Tommy grabbed his hand and pulled him toward the door. "Not yet, but you're working on it. Now let's go party. Just think, tomorrow this time you'll be on your way to seeing your boy."

Ru thought of Adam and couldn't help but smile.

"See, there's the pretty. Let's go get our groove on."

CHAPTER 12

ADAM had called Ru after dinner, gotten his voice mail, and begged him to call back as soon as he could. Two hours later and no return call, Adam texted him. It wasn't until after he'd crawled in bed and dozed off that the phone finally rang. He answered it without looking at the screen. No one else would call this late.

"Sorry," Ru said right away.

"S'okay. Are you okay?"

"Yeah, just tired. I feel like I'm trying to cram so much into every day just to get back to you sooner."

And just like that Adam felt guilty. "Don't overwork yourself for me. I'll still be here when you get back."

"I keep having nightmares of you meeting someone else. Or that big football jock I saw you running with pushing me away and claiming you're his."

"Nate? No way. You have nothing to worry about." Adam smiled into the phone. "Can I see you? Where are you? Can you take a picture?"

"Ha! I look awful."

"Please."

"Okay. Hold on a sec." Ru disappeared from the phone for a moment and then came back, "Just sent it. Don't say I didn't warn you. And you need to return the favor. I can only imagine how heavenly you look all sleepy and warm in bed."

Adam opened the image and smiled at his boy. Ru did look tired, eyes a little red, but his hair was spiked and he had dark eyeliner on. It was different. He still looked good. He just didn't look like Ru, more like some celebrity from the cover of a glamour magazine.

Adam's own picture back was of him smiling, propped up against the pillows in almost complete darkness. If not for the flash, it would have been a worthless picture. As it was, Ru laughed. "You could have turned a light on."

"It's almost 2:00 a.m. My parents would have a fit."

"Sorry. I don't want to get you in trouble."

"You won't. So hey, listen, um, I talked to my mom and dad, and they are okay with you coming and staying overnight on Saturday. I thought maybe if you want to you could come here instead of going to that condo, and then we can do something on Sunday. I mean, only if you want to." *Way to take over his life, dumbass*, Adam reprimanded himself. Not like the guy had asked to stay with you. Maybe Ru liked the condo and having people drive him everywhere.

"You sure that's okay with your parents?"

"Yeah, you just have to stay in the spare bedroom. No sharing."

"So much for that talk about condoms?" He sounded amused.

"Yeah, so much. I think it will be different when they meet you. I think they'll like you."

"And if they don't?"

"Ru...."

"It's okay, baby. I'd love to stay with you. My flight comes in pretty late. I think sometime around eleven. I don't know if I can catch an earlier one."

"You just going to have your driver bring you here?"

"Yeah. You'll wait up?"

"I'll wait forever," Adam told him honestly.

The next day Adam was a bundle of nerves. He journaled for two hours before having to get up and move. His mom set about cleaning the guest room top to bottom, washing sheets and vacuuming. Adam tried to help, but after the fourth time of getting in her way, she banished him to the living room. He almost felt like his skin couldn't contain him anymore. He needed to see Ru. And if he couldn't he would start throwing things.

"I just want everything to be perfect for Ru."

"It will be," his mom assured him. "You just have to let me finish picking up. Do you have any homework?"

"No." Adam always finished it in study hall if he could.

"Why don't you go for a run," she suggested. Great suggestion, only there was like a foot of snow on the ground, and it wasn't even November yet. "Josiah, take him to the community center."

Adam's dad looked up from the paper he'd been thumbing through all morning. He seemed to study Adam for a second and then nodded. "Get changed."

"I don't know….," Adam began, feeling itchy and just irritated.

His dad shooed him upstairs. Adam put on his running things, new pants, dry shoes and socks, in some weird fog. Ru just needed to get here, because Adam was going to go nuts without him. By the time Adam got back downstairs, his dad had changed too, and then they were off to the community center. The place had a giant, half-mile indoor track on the second floor. It always smelled like cleaner and rubber since the actual track was made from recycled tires. Adam liked the bounciness of it.

His dad hadn't even had time to strip out of his coat before Adam abandoned him and took to stretching. But Adam let him set the pace, and together they ran. A little over a year ago, his dad had first brought Adam here and told him they were going to run. Adam had laughed then, feeling it some grand joke. At the time he had been in his pissy teen stage, angry at the world, wearing black and writing on brand new clothes to ruin them just because he figured if he was angry all the time, the rest of the world should be.

And then his dad had shown Adam what it was to run. Sure, Adam could outrun him now. His legs were longer and well used to moving for long periods of time, but his dad kept up better than Nate ever had. When Adam bumped up the speed, his dad pushed to match, and they just kept going. Others came in and set slower paces; some just walked, staying to the outer edges while they flew by. He and his dad never really talked when they came there. This time was no different.

When Adam got tired, his dad pushed him to keep moving. Someone handed him a bottle of water, and Adam gulped it down but didn't stop. He never knew how it was his dad could run so long. Did he go on lunch break from work? How was it he could make even Adam, who was used to running for hours a day, work so hard?

Sweat was pouring off Adam, and his lungs burned by the time his dad eased them into a slow, just-above-walking pace. They headed to the showers, and Adam realized he had been so out of his head before coming that he hadn't packed a bag of clean clothes. Yet his dad stood there with a duffle, already showered and changed, handing over the bag with a small smile.

"Do you need more?" his dad asked quietly, about the running, not the clothes. What he was really asking was "Is your head clear yet?"

It wasn't until that moment that Adam realized he needed the track more than it needed him. "I'm okay. Sorry about this morning. Sometimes…." Sometimes he just didn't feel normal in his own skin. Adam threw on the clean clothes and followed his dad out the door. If he wasn't going to run for football or for track, he was still going to have to run, if just to keep sane.

Instead of going home, his dad took him to lunch. They sat near the fireplace at the restaurant, waiting for their sandwiches and soup. His dad smiled and just looked happy to be there. When the food came, they ate in silence, enjoying the meal and letting it recharge their worn bodies.

When Adam pushed away his plate, his dad picked up the bag he'd brought in with him and pulled out a book. "I want you to read this, Adam. Not because you have to write a paper or because your teacher requests you to read it. I want you to read it because these very things may just happen to you."

Adam took the book from him and flipped it over to read the back. It was a book about a gay guy who had been bullied about being gay until he committed suicide. And suddenly Adam didn't want to know the story because it scared him.

His dad put his hand over Adam's. "You don't have to take it to school with you. You can just read it at home. But I want you to read it. And if anyone starts to do to you things like what happened to this boy, you need to come to me right away, okay?"

Adam nodded and glared at the book in his hand. They went home, but it was just after one, so there were still hours before Ru was to arrive. He wasn't answering any of Adam's texts, and Adam had nothing to do, so he sat down and began to read the damn book. It was horrible. A train wreck in slow motion, yet he couldn't stop reading and comparing it to his life. He'd seen some of those very same things happen to Bas; some had even happened to him. Adam feared for the young man in the story, even knowing what was going to happen.

When Bobby died, Adam cried. He thought about Bas and some of the other kids who never really fit in. Not everyone could coast like Adam had been. And really, why should they? Adam had sort of lived in this fantasy world where nothing could touch him, until he met Ru, even when guys like the jockstraps bugged him.

Adam realized Ru would probably not fit in either. With his painted black nails, skater-punk hair, and infectious loud laughter, he'd be alienated, teased, bullied. No wonder he let himself be so alone. He had no idea of the horribly unforgiving world that would just eat him up.

Adam cast the book aside, knowing he would never forget Bobby's story and how it had opened his eyes to things he had worked so hard to ignore. He thought of all the things he should have done—should be doing—when some of the other kids started to bother Bas. But he still had that odd gut-wrenching fear.

Dinner was silent. His mom made chicken and steamed veggies with a light curry sauce. It would heat up well later when Ru's plane finally landed. They didn't talk because Adam still had too much going on in his head from reading that book. There were things he wanted to ask his parents and yet didn't, because he didn't want to know. The best thing about being a teenager is really thinking that you know everything and can conquer anything. The worst is finding that it's all a lie.

His mom and dad headed to bed just after ten. Adam sat up, watching *Teen Wolf* and thinking it was pretty hard being just a teen;

add becoming a wolf once a month, and the average guy would be screwed. He must have dozed because a hesitant knock jolted him awake like a shot from a cannon. He jumped up and headed to the door.

Ru stood there, looking like himself again, only tired, backpack and guitar case in hand. Adam motioned him inside, and Ru waved to the car idling at the end of the drive, which then drove off. After Adam closed the door, they just stood there for a moment, staring at each other. He was rememorizing the edges of Ru's face, his pretty slanted eyes, the long lashes, thick lips. Adam leaned forward, and they kissed. Just like each time before, it was like angels singing. Perfect.

A minute later Adam was crying, clinging to Ru like he was all he had left in this world. Ru whispered soft words that really didn't make any sense since Adam was so lost in his own head. Here Ru was in front of him, and yet Adam was terrified of anything happening to him. He had fallen hard. The sort of things he read in books about meeting that person and just finding that you can't even see the world beyond them anymore—those stories had always seemed so dumb when he'd had to read them for school. Fantasy. Until now.

Adam didn't know how it happened, but somehow they ended up in his room. Ru curled around him on the bed, and Adam just clung to him. Ru piled the blankets over them and kicked off his shoes but was otherwise clothed. A flash of panic had Adam shoving away from Ru when he thought of what his parents would say if they found them in the same bed together.

"Shh, baby. It's okay. Let me get you calmed down, and then I'll go to the spare room. I promise. Shh." His words were so sweet, his breath warm on Adam's neck, arms a comforting weight. Adam's shield. His barrier. Adam fell asleep to his soft words and strong arms.

CHAPTER 13

BEFORE he left for Minnesota, Ru had spent a good part of the day doing interviews for magazines and appearing on a few radio shows, where he performed his new song "Start Something" acoustically. On his way out for lunch, Tommy picked him up, and they headed to the best sandwich shop in town. By "in town," it really meant an out of the way place where people rarely recognized him.

They had one bodyguard with them, which Ru's label had hired before his first performance that week. The man was big, built like a linebacker but dressed casual, undercover. Ru hadn't said more than a handful of words to the man, and the guard had shown a great deal of discretion and watchfulness of the people who surrounded them.

Tommy yanked his sandwich free of the paper wrapping and took a huge bite, dripping mayonnaise and oil everywhere.

"Wow, messy much?" Ru teased. His was whole wheat, skinny bread with fat-free turkey, light Swiss, and pickles.

"You're just jealous," Tommy said, mouth full.

"Yeah, a little. But you're the one who's gonna be practicing choreographed AJ moves all night feeling like a bloated whale."

"Ouch."

Ru took a bite of his sandwich. It was good, flavorful, even without all the extra calories added. "Maybe I'll take up running."

Tommy laughed, took a swallow of his drink then laughed a little harder. "You run? From the paps, maybe. So you're going to be staying with your boy tonight."

"Subtle."

"In his folk's house. No playing—that's weird."

"Seriously, when was the last time you got laid? 'Cause your obsession with my sex life is getting a little old." Ru picked at his sandwich. He planned on letting Adam set the pace since the guy was a virgin. It was only fair, and he remembered all too well what it felt like to be pressured.

"I need a girl first. One who isn't going to run to the media the second I ask her out."

"I thought you had a black book of one-night stands?"

Tommy sighed and pushed his plate away. "I did. Except half of them are calling the paps with info about my sexual prowess now and saying they had no clue I was gay."

"But you're not gay," Ru pointed out.

"It'd probably be easier to get laid if I was."

Ru shook his head and made a crude gesture with his hand.

"Dude, that only goes so far, you know."

"Been working for me." Ru smiled at his BFF.

"Yeah, while you fantasize about being with Adam, right? Well, I need someone to fantasize about being with too. Just 'cause I'm straight doesn't mean it doesn't get old." Tommy looked wistfully out the window. "Some of my old friends from high school are getting married in the next few weeks."

"Is that what you want? To get married?"

"Not right this second but someday, you know." He waved his hands at Ru. "I want what you have."

"What I have? You mean the solo recording contract?"

"No. I mean that goofy look you get on your face anytime you think of him. Or if I say his name you smile. The past week has been a total turnaround from where you were. I was worried for a while there. Didn't know if you were going to make it through leaving the group. But even when you were with Kris, I don't remember you being this happy. I want that."

Ru grabbed Tommy's hand and squeezed. He hadn't realized how lonely his friend had probably been. "I bet there's an Amanda waiting for you somewhere in Minnesota."

"Amanda?"

"First girl name I could think of that sounds close to Adam."

They both laughed.

"So are you staying here tonight?" Ru asked.

Tommy nodded. "Doing some studio stuff tomorrow with VG. Might fly out sometime next week, though. You going to be in the condo during the week?"

"Yeah. I'll try to work on new songs. Did you know Adam's journals are brilliant? I've gotten another half-dozen ideas out of them. I'm hoping he lets me read some of his older stuff. I may have been around the world a few times, but sometimes I feel like he's got a better grasp of it than I do." Ru picked up his sandwich and finished it off. "I bet he'd have a huge following if he had a blog or something."

"You could bring it up to him."

"Nah, his parents have some strict Internet rules."

"Which is probably why he has no idea who you are."

Ru sighed. "I'll try to work on telling him this weekend."

"How do you think he'll take it?"

He had no idea. In fact, Ru was more than a little afraid to tell Adam. "Katie said to try to keep it low. She warned me that Adam probably doesn't have thick skin like us. But you don't have to tell me twice how nasty the media can get."

"Speaking of which, wave, we've got paps." Tommy raised his hand and faked a smile while looking out the window. A half-dozen photographers began snapping pictures.

"So much for a quiet lunch. How did they find this place anyway?"

A limo pulled up beside the curb, and the driver got out to open the back door. Ru's stomach did a flip-flop that nearly had him running for the garbage can as AJ got out of the car. He posed a dozen times, smile huge, golden blond hair perfectly styled. He had a mass of bodyguards around him, who moved as a wall to open the door for him and let him inside.

"What the hell does he want?" Tommy grumbled.

"Maybe it was just a coincidence—" Ru began but stopped as AJ headed right to their table and sat down like he owned the place. "Hi, AJ."

"Well if it isn't the prodigal son and his little bitch."

"Fuck you, AJ," Tommy said.

AJ's smile didn't falter at all. He leaned in close to Ru. "You think you're so hot."

"I don't know what you're talking about. I've just been promoting my new song, 'Start Something.' Can't help it if my manager knows what she's doing." Ru sat back and folded his arms across his chest. "If it makes you happy, I plan on going back into the studio for the next week or so and not doing anymore interviews until I have half my debut album completed."

"Do you realize what you are doing to Tommy's career?" AJ demanded.

"What the fuck, man. He's not doing anything!" Tommy protested.

"Shut up, Foster. Just because you don't want to see it doesn't mean I can't see it. Everyone thinks you're gay too." AJ waved a hand at the guards, who cleared out an area of the restaurant so no one could hear them talking. God forbid someone hear one of AJ's infamous rants. He smiled and looked like the perfect gentleman for all the cameras across the street.

"We are a boy band, AJ. Everyone thinks we're all gay. We all knew that going in," Tommy grabbed his plate and headed to the garbage, trying to end the conversation.

AJ got into Ru's face, still smiling like he was the sweetest thing on the planet. "You're screwing up his life. Just because you're a pervert doesn't mean he has to be. You couldn't even let the media die down before going all Glam Queen on late night. Who the fuck do you think you are?"

"Ryunoski Nakimura. The guy who wrote all the songs that made you famous. The voice that made Vocal Growth a legend. Now I'm doing it just for me, while you flounder, because you don't matter to me anymore. Now if you'll excuse me, I have an interview to get ready for." Ru got up. AJ rose with him and put his hand on his chest. "Don't touch, you may get the gay," Ru growled at him and stalked out of the restaurant, Tommy and their guard on his heels. He jammed his oversized sunglasses down onto his face and stepped into the flash of lights. Ru didn't bother to smile as he got into the car and made his way to his next appointment for the day. All he could think about was getting back to the quiet life he'd found with Adam in freezing Minnesota.

When he finally stepped off the plane and made his way to see Adam, most of the trouble of his lunchtime confrontation had faded away. Things were looking up, until he walked in the door of Adam's small suburban home, kissed the guy, and then had to watch Adam fall apart. When Adam had asked him to stay the weekend, Ru was sure he could fly if he needed too. When the door opened and Adam stood there, looking so wonderful, even with his hair askew and lines of sleep on his face, Ru just wanted to wrap himself up in the guy and stay forever.

Then the tears started. From what Ru gathered from Adam's incoherent mumblings, it was something about a book and not being strong enough to stand up to all the bullies. All Ru knew was that Adam had a huge heart that absorbed way too much of the pain of the world. When Adam had finally fallen asleep, he'd crossed the room to Adam's computer, found some recent journal entries, and read through the past few days to try to better understand him.

When Ru logged off the computer, he had a better sense of where Adam's head was, but little idea how to fix it. He set the alarm on his phone to wake him up fairly early so he could find the guestroom before Adam's parents rose in the morning. Then he texted Tommy. *How can I protect someone from the whole world?*

Tommy's text back was almost instantaneous. *Wears his heart on his sleeve?*

Yeah.

Dunno. Been trying to help u with that for years.

Ru sighed and curled up beside Adam. He settled down close enough for his forehead to rest against Adam's, to breathe the same small space of air.

CHAPTER 14

THE smell of syrup roused Adam from bed pretty early that Sunday. The light had barely begun to peek through the window with its gray overcast paleness. His head hurt, probably from the crying, and Adam had a flash of embarrassed horror when he realized what an idiot he had been in front Ru. The absence of his weight in Adam's bed made his heart nearly skip a beat. Had Ru left? Was he so disgusted with Adam's waterworks that he took off in the middle of the night?

Adam threw off the blankets, did a quick clean up in the bathroom, and headed downstairs to see if Ru was still there. *Please let him still be there.*

In the kitchen both of Adam's parents were awake, but there was no sign of Ru. He left them to fill plates with stacks of pancakes to head to the spare room. Ru was sprawled out on the bed in nothing but his boxers. Blankets thrown off and arms flung across the bed, it looked like he'd just fallen there in an exhausted heap. Adam wanted to just crawl into bed with him, wrap his arms around Ru's chest, and snuggle them up into the blankets for the rest of the day.

"Come eat," Adam's dad whispered. "Let him sleep since he got in so late. You and I can hit the gym, and hopefully he'll be up by the time we get back. Your mom will make sure he eats."

Adam didn't really want to leave Ru there alone with his mom. Maybe Ru would wake up while they were eating breakfast. A half-dozen pancakes, two eggs, and three slices of bacon later, Adam was full and ready to go. His dad gave him time to run upstairs, change, and check on Ru again, who was still sound asleep.

When Adam hesitated to go for the third time, his mom thrust a piece of paper and a pencil into his hand. "Write him a quick note. If he wakes up before you get back, I'll give it to him."

Adam sighed and quickly penned, *Went to run. BBS.* With that they left. The gym was emptier that day than it had been the day before, probably due to it being not quite seven on a Sunday. Adam and his dad started out faster, just a few warm-ups, and then set a quick pace. He was sleepy, but that wore off after the second lap.

"Focus on your breathing," his dad told him, his not even strained yet. "It's early, but your body knows what to do."

And it did. Adam channeled all his mental focus into breathing, letting his body move like it knew how to. The walls soared by in a blurred circle. Eventually his dad stopped and mumbled something about getting something to drink. But Adam just kept going, feeling the burn in his lungs, the heat of his legs, the weight of his spine, and the soft rhythm of his breath.

His pushed all his frustrations of the past few days out into the run. Like cleansing his body of toxins, he released it all with each breath. The worry about Bas, his fear of having Ru walk away, and even his own insecurity about his future—he just dropped it all. It took some time to finally free himself and just run with his mind clear and completely unfettered, but when he found that place, he didn't want to stop.

Sometime later someone reached out as he approached the entrance area, holding out a bottle of water. Adam expected it to be his dad, but when the half-second glance didn't register his familiar blond hair he had to look again and went sprawling on his face. Adam didn't think he had ever wiped out so spectacularly. His legs flew over his head a few times and when the forward motion finally stopped, he lay on his back, staring up at the ceiling, world spinning and knees stinging.

"I'm so sorry!" Ru knelt down beside him, and then Adam's dad appeared on the other side. "Your dad said you needed some water. I didn't want to distract you. I was trying to do it how you see them do it for people who are running marathons." Adam blinked at Ru, amused by the way his eyes got really big and bright when he worried. His dad put a towel under Adam's head, and then his mom appeared with another set of towels. "Your knees are bleeding pretty badly."

Adam peered down at them and sighed at the heavy gobs of blood that poured from the scrapes. No wonder it burned. His mom began washing them gently as one of the gym employees arrived with a first aid bag. "I sort of felt like Wile E. Coyote when he chases the Road Runner off a cliff, suspended in air for a minute before gravity kicks in. It was cool," Adam told them.

"Did you hit your head?" his dad asked. Ru gripped Adam's hand as the medic moved around to shine a light in his eyes.

"He needs water," the man said. His hands ran over Adam's neck, listening to his pulse and searching the vertebrae for signs of damage. Another medic appeared this one female. She took over working on Adam's knees, using something with a horrible sting to clean them, and then bandaged them. "Roll over onto your side," the man instructed. When Adam did, the man examined his spine for any sign of damage.

"I'm okay," Adam told them all. "Just feel really stupid."

His dad helped him sit up, and Ru handed Adam the bottle of water. "Drink, please."

He gulped down all twelve ounces without stopping for a breath. His muscles were starting to ache. After all that running, they would really hurt if he didn't stretch them properly. Except his knees had giant white bandages on them. The jogging pants he had brought to put on over the shorts probably wouldn't fit.

The medics declared he wasn't permanently damaged, which made his face burn. When they helped him up, all he could do was bury his face against Ru's shirt and cling to the man. Ru wore just a T-shirt and a pair of sweats, but it didn't look like he'd hit any of the exercise machines. Adam, however, needed a shower something fierce. He stunk.

His dad ended up helping him, which was awkward. They tied some plastic bags around Adam's knees, but the water and soap got in anyway and hurt pretty bad. Before his knees were rewrapped, Adam finally got to see the damage. Major road rash. Once it scabbed over it was going to be hard to move, even harder to run. Adam sighed. His dad packed up his stuff.

"I'm going to take the bags out to the car. I'll be back in a minute to help with your shoes," he told Adam. Adam could probably get his shoes on himself, but it seemed like a long way to bend. Exhaustion was starting to settle in, but he fought the heaviness of his eyelids, not wanting to lose more time with Ru.

The track pants did fit over the bandages, but his knees stuck out like giant marshmallows had been shoved into the legs. Ru showed up again as Adam was pulling on his sweatshirt. Ru whipped a comb out of his pocket and gently ran it through Adam's hair. A spot on the back left side of his head hurt a little, like when he'd banged his head into the door or a table by accident. He rubbed the spot lightly.

"You scared the crap out of me, Adam," Ru whispered.

Adam thought he meant for leaving the house without him. "I'm sorry. I left a note. Did my mom give it to you?"

"Yeah, that's why we came here. Your mom drove us over when your dad sent a text saying you were still running. We figured we would meet up with you and have lunch once you were done." He stared off into space for a minute. "I meant that fall. I think my heart stopped while you were tumbling. It was almost like you were flying while you were running. But I don't think you were seeing anything around you. I shouldn't have tried to break your concentration." He squeezed Adam's hand. "It's almost noon."

"Oh no!" How had he wasted half the day, a day he should have been spending with Ru? "I didn't realize...."

"It's okay. Your mom and I got here around ten. I did a little walking on the treadmill and some basic weight lifting. This gym is nice, having the equipment right on the edge of the track. I could watch you the whole time. Didn't realize I'd done twice my normal reps on everything. Being with you is going to make my personal trainer very happy." Ru leaned forward and kissed Adam's cheek. "I was just pumping iron, losing track of the counts over and over. Too busy watching you."

Adam rested his forehead against Ru's and just let the man's breath brush across his face in sweet warmth. "Sometimes I need to run. Just to clear my head."

"Your dad told me. Once I'd got showered up and found you still running, we went downstairs to grab a smoothie. He's a pretty good guy."

"He wasn't weird with you or anything?"

"He didn't threaten to break my arms or anything, if that's what you mean." Ru brushed Adam's hair out of his face. "Asked me a lot of questions. Makes sense. He's your dad. He wants to make sure I'm not some jerk."

Adam sighed sweetly when Ru grabbed his hand and let their fingers slide together.

"We're going to Dimitri's for lunch. Your dad says the carbs and some extra protein will do you good. Food first, then maybe a nap. I think they might even let us nap together as long as we leave the door open." Ru let go of Adam's hand and bent over to help him into his shoes. Heat rushed to Adam's cheeks when he thought about curling up with Ru in his bed.

"I can do that," Adam complained.

Ru just shook his head, tied each shoe tightly, then rose to his feet and offered Adam his hand. "Let's go eat. You're still pretty pale. I think we need to get more water and some food in you."

When Adam stood up, he *was* a little shaky. His dad reappeared, this time with a couple of bottles of water. His mom met them outside the locker room, but his dad had already pulled the SUV around. They all got in, Adam and Ru in the very back so they could sit together. Ru put the blanket from the day before around Adam after he was sure the younger man was buckled in, then handed him the water. "Two of these before we get to the restaurant, okay?"

Adam nodded and drank, happy to have his hand in Ru's grasp and the man's thigh pressed to his, even if the bandages on his knees felt a little weird. His mom and dad spoke to each other, but not in a way that made him think they were talking about them, for which Adam was grateful.

When the group arrived, the place was pretty much empty. Guess pizza wasn't a big lunch on Sunday. They got a booth, Ru and Adam on one side, Adam's folks on the other. Adam didn't need to look at the menu. He was craving meat something fierce and probably needed the vitamins in veggies, so he would eat just about anything.

"Anything you don't like, Ru?" his dad asked.

"I'm good with anything except anchovies."

"I don't like anchovies either," Adam told him.

Dimitri himself waited on their table, smiling and patting Ru on the back while chatting up Adam's parents. They got two large pizzas with heaping veggies and four kinds of meat. By the time the food arrived, Adam was so hungry he could have eaten the plate. He probably ate half a pizza by himself. When he was finally full, he leaned on Ru and practically fell asleep on his shoulder.

"Let's get you home for a nap. 'Kay, baby?" Ru asked.

"'Kay." Adam let Ru lead him back to the car but really didn't remember the ride home. When he awoke later, he was in bed, Ru wrapped around him; the blankets snug around them like someone had tucked them in. Adam snapped a few pictures with his cell phone of Ru sleeping, loving the way his dark lashes looked against his peach cheeks. He looked very young when sleeping, and Adam didn't want to disturb him, but knew by the set of the sun through the window and the time on his iPhone that it was getting late.

His mom poked her head through the open doorway. Adam blinked up at her, waiting for her to call for his dad since he was in bed with Ru, but she just smiled. "Dinner's almost ready. You should both get up or you won't sleep tonight."

"Okay," Adam told her, then had to ask, "Aren't you mad?"

She shook her head. "Nope." Then she was gone.

Ru opened his sleepy eyes and rewarded Adam with a tiny grin. "Hey, baby."

Adam leaned forward and kissed him. "Not sure about the baby thing. I like when you call me anything. It's just weird to hear 'baby.'"

Ru returned Adam's kiss with sweet ones of his own. "How about Sport? Champ? Honey?"

"How about Adam?" Adam teased.

"Okay. Anything you want."

Adam wanted to cuddle with Ru a while longer, but his folks weren't having that. His dad popped in five minutes later to make sure they were awake. And they were, though they had been kissing. Just sitting up on the bed, legs crossed, kissing like nothing else mattered. Adam's dad cleared his throat. They pulled away from each other, shared a guilty glance, and then burst out laughing. His dad walked away shaking his head and calling out, "Downstairs for food, now."

They both finally yanked themselves from the warm confines of the bed and down to dinner. Ru talked about his homeschooling and how he loved music. Adam's mom invited him to play, but Ru got all embarrassed. She let it go with a "maybe next time."

Adam had to hide a smile behind his cup. They were going to let Ru stay over again. They liked him. Adam's dad started a conversation with Ru about the changes to rock music over the last decade. Music was a topic that animated Ru. His hands flew around wildly, his expressions over the top, all his emotions on his face and seeming to pour up through his skin from the mere mention. Everything about him was so uninhibited, but it made sense because he hadn't attended an actual school since he was ten. He hadn't learned to hide what he felt or put on a mask. When he laughed, they all laughed. And no one scolded Adam when he gripped Ru's hand under the table.

When it was time for Ru to go, Adam walked him to the door. The dark town car idled at the end of the walk. Adam sighed. Was it really over so soon? Ru kissed him on the cheek. "After school tomorrow? Do you want me to pick you up?"

They planned to go to the gym each day so Adam could run. Ru had promised Adam's dad he'd keep Adam from running himself into the ground while he was there and would have him home by dinner. Since Adam planned to quit the football team, it made sense. He glanced at his parents. His dad just shrugged. "Sure."

"'Kay." Ru kissed Adam again, this time just a light brush on the lips, and then he was headed down the walkway. Adam waited until Ru got in and the car drove off before shutting the door. Now would start the countdown once again. How many hours until Adam could see him again?

His dad patted him on the back. "He seems like a nice boy. But don't let your grades suffer over this relationship. Life is about finding a balance. Can you do that?"

Adam looked at him and thought about it. "Yeah. I think so. I mean, I can't wait to see him again, but the faster the school day goes, the sooner I'll get to see him. And if I'm actually working in class, studying, doing homework, the day will feel like it's going faster."

"That's my boy."

CHAPTER 15

RU RETURNED to the empty condo after the whirlwind weekend feeling energized. He thought about that morning and Adam's spill. Ru had feared he'd caused Adam to break his neck and reprimanded himself a million times. At least his discussion with Adam's dad had gone smoothly. The questions were basic, just about his family and how he ended up taking care of himself. Ru had been relieved when the man didn't dig too deeply, but also disappointed because that would have been an easy way to tell Adam about his fame. Though the conversation had been somewhat terrifying.

He had sat across from Adam's dad, who told him to call him Josiah. "Thank you, sir. Josiah, I mean," Ru said.

"I know you and Adam have just met, but I wanted to have a chance to talk with you privately. Get a feel for your intentions and tell you a little about Adam," the man said.

"I really like Adam." Ru worried Adam's father would say they couldn't see each other anymore.

"He has matured a little slower than a lot of other boys. Slower than I did myself. He's still very innocent."

Ru nodded, knowing all too well what Mr. Corbin meant. "I understand. I have no intention of pushing him into anything he's not ready for. Adam means a lot to me. I've never felt this way about anyone before…."

"But you are also very young," Josiah pointed out.

Not really, but Ru didn't protest. "I had a boyfriend before Adam."

"And were you safe with this other boy?"

Was he asking about protection? "Yes, mostly. And when the relationship ended, I got tested. Have been tested twice since, actually. I found out he was cheating on me. It made me pretty paranoid for a while."

Josiah grabbed Ru's hand and squeezed it. "I'm sorry that happened to you. And I'm sure you can understand that I want to avoid the same thing from happening to Adam. He's got a very big heart, and the last thing I want to see is it broken."

Ru nodded, agreeing completely. "I can't make promises, but I am really hopeful that this thing between us is something that's going to last. I mean, it feels amazing. Just holding his hand makes me feel like I can conquer the world. I never felt that before. Not even with Kris. He was my ex." Ru sighed and looked away as one of the staff brought over their smoothies. So far no one had recognized him, or if they had, they were being very quiet about it, but the place was filling up fast.

"World domination aside, I can tell you're pretty in tune to Adam. And him to you. He says you're not close with your family, wants to show you his because he's happy and feels like he's loved. I understand that. I just want you to take it slow. Give him space to grow. You both are so very young."

"I won't push him. That promise I will make. And I want him to be whoever he is growing up to be. I don't know if you've read some of his journals, but he's an amazing writer. His take on the world is so subtle, realistic, sweet, and yet harsh. I've learned more from him the past week about living than I think I have in the last seventeen years of actual life." Ru took a sip of his smoothie. Not bad for something under 200 calories. He wished they were upstairs watching Adam run. "It's probably too soon to say it, but I'm pretty sure I'm in love with him."

Josiah smiled, squeezed Ru's hand again, and let the topic go. "So how is it you ended up on your own?"

"Hard questions first, right?" Ru asked and sighed. "My dad really pushed me when I was young. I learned all about music, piano and guitar, was writing and performing by the time I was six. When I started earning money, he got pushier. But I thought I could trust him. I mean, he was my dad, you know?"

Mr. Corbin just nodded.

"I knew I was different. Not just because I was so focused, but because I never noticed girls the way the other boys did. What little time I had that wasn't devoted to schoolwork or practice, I thought about what it meant to be so different. It really scared me. I thought sharing it with him would help."

"You told him you're gay?"

Ru nodded. "I was eleven. On the verge of great things but struggling to grasp some sense of self. I thought my dad would be proud I was doing so much, and that I knew who I was. Only he wasn't. To this day, I don't remember much other than the disgust on his face. I know he yelled at me, called me things, demanded I hide this part of me, even tried to convince me that I was confused. I can still hear bits and pieces of his words, but it was that look that did it for me. I knew he'd never accept me. No matter how hard I worked, how much money or fame I had, he would never love me. Probably never did love me." And Ru felt the hot burning of tears in his eyes. He sniffed and ground his teeth together, trying to hold them back. "He and my mom had divorced years before because he was so laser-focused on my career, and she just wanted to be some rich man's wife. So when it all came down, he walked out."

"The two of you haven't talked since?"

"No." Ru looked up into the light, hating that talking about his dad had made him feel so weak. "I thought maybe he'd call or something. But about two months later, he sent me documentation that made me independent." Ru waved his hand. "It's all about the money anyway. I can hire people to take care of me. So I guess I don't need parents. My mom shows up when she wants money."

"You do need parents. Parents aren't there just to provide monetary support. They are there to hold you when you're sad, tell you when you're doing something stupid to try to keep you from getting hurt, and love you even when you think no one else will." Mr. Corbin wrapped his arms around Ru, and despite trying so hard not to cry, Ru let it all go, sobbing into the older man's arms. This was what having a dad was supposed to feel like.

After a short time, Ru finally pulled away, rubbing his eyes with the sleeves of his shirt. "Sorry. I guess I know why Adam thinks so highly of you guys."

Mr. Corbin patted Ru's hand. "You need anything, you call me, okay? People shouldn't abandon their children just because things didn't turn out the way they want. Nothing in life works that way. Heck, Clara and I got married thinking we'd have a dozen kids, only to find out her body is too frail for that."

Ru nodded. "Yeah, life kind of disappoints a lot, right?"

"Only if you let it. We've got one amazing kid. That's all that matters. And we've certainly got room for another." Mr. Corbin patted Ru's hand again and then went on to ask general questions about his life in California. Whatever Ru had said must have gained him Mr. Corbin's approval, because the man let him go back upstairs alone while he went off to find his wife.

When he was alone in Tommy's condo that evening, Ru picked up his guitar and began strumming randomly and just playing through chords. His body was tired since he'd worked out harder than he ever had in his life without even realizing it. He sent a text to Tommy before returning to the condo, asking if his friend would be joining him soon. The place was just so big and lonely without Adam or Tommy to brighten it up.

After a while Ru sang "Starting Something" again and began practicing the two other tunes he'd written. Adam had given him an entire memory stick with journal ramblings to read. A year's worth, he'd said. And when Ru opened up the folder, it was a lot of material, but just as meticulously sorted and cataloged as everything else was. Ru had read through a few things in the car.

After a few minutes of playing, he made his way into the tiny studio just to queue up some of the background tracks. He had a few ideas and wanted to play through them; after all, it would be hours before he could see Adam again.

The next morning he Skyped Tommy bright and early, pinging the man until he got out of bed. "Is AJ letting you sleep all day?" Ru asked him.

Tommy groaned. "I wish. Gotta be at the studio at one to work on some moves. I tried talking to the label about the songs yesterday. Oh, did I tell you we got handed a stack that AJ chose? And guess who gets most of the solos?"

"I'm sorry, man."

"No worries. Talk to me. You woke me up for a reason."

"Can we do this"—Ru motioned to the two of them on the laptop—"and work on music? I've got some songs that I think could use some help."

"You know I don't really do anything other than ask you questions, right?"

"But it makes my songs better 'cause it's stuff I wasn't thinking about before."

"Okay, okay, beat me over the head already." Tommy sighed and pulled the tablet back with him as he lay back down on his bed. "Let's hear it."

They worked on the songs together, nailing down a full instrumental—one Ru had no idea where to begin on the lyrics—before Tommy had to go get ready for his own job. Ru had spent the few hours in between when Tommy left and time to pick Adam up by reading through Adam's journals, which sometimes were truly incoherent and other times pure genius. He wondered if the changes correlated to when Adam could run and when he couldn't. He'd highlighted some things and started a file of thoughts, phrases, and ideas he liked best and could try to cull for songs later. And while Ru wasn't looking forward to spending time working out, he did want to see Adam pretty badly by the time 4:00 p.m. rolled around.

"So you walk on the treadmill," Adam said when they had changed and headed up to the main workout area. "Let's do a little jog on the track to get your heart up."

"As long as you do some lifting with me, I'll try to jog with you," Ru offered as a compromise. He spent a lot of time working on his back, abs, shoulders, and arms. While he would never get the definition in his abs he wanted, he had great core strength. Adam was all amazing gluts and strong calves. Not that Ru had a problem with either of those things.

"Sure. We'll start slow." And so they ran together. Ru pushed himself hard to keep up with Adam's much subdued pace. He worried a lot when his lungs started to burn. Would that be bad for his voice? He slowed to a stop, and Adam walked back toward him, keeping his legs moving. "Don't just stop, your muscles will get tight. The charley horse from that is awful."

"Can't breathe," Ru panted.

"Oh. Forgot about that. Let's work through it together, but walk while we do it, okay? I'll teach you how to breathe right."

"There's a special way?" Ru asked as he began moving his feet. His side ached, and he felt like he was breathing through a straw.

"First, stop fighting so hard for air. Your body knows what it needs. Take long breaths. Inhale, deep, and exhale, hoooo," Adam said, huffing out a long breath.

Ru did his best to mimic him. After a few minutes of walking and breathing, he began to feel better, and Adam bumped them back into a run. This time they kept going until Ru's legs trembled. It was odd how focusing on the breathing took his mind off the work his body was going through. He just moved, talked through each breath in his head, and followed Adam's lead. But it was Adam who stopped them and led him over to the mats for a stretch.

"Always stretch after running. Here are a few I do to keep from stiffening up." He went through a few different poses that almost looked like yoga. Ru followed somewhat clumsily. His body was warm and fluid feeling. He wondered if he could always get this weird adrenaline push when he ran. "Now some weights. Do you target muscles?"

"My personal trainer usually tells me what to do," Ru admitted, somewhat embarrassed.

"And when he's not around?" Adam asked.

Ru shrugged. "I don't really like working out."

"Okay, then." Adam nodded, more to himself than to anything Ru had to say. "Let's target different muscle groups on different days. What area do you want to work on most?"

"My abs," Ru said. "I've never been able to get rid of my cupcake top."

Adam frowned, looking over Ru like he was searching for something. "We'll work on the fitness ball today, then. Let me show you some good exercises to work the whole core." He led Ru over to a couple of big yoga balls and demonstrated some things Ru had probably done before. When they finished their workout, Ru was tired but not ready to part ways yet. They headed down to the showers together, and since Adam was a little shy about getting into the shower with Ru watching, they both made their way into separate, private shower stations and kept covered.

Ru wasn't used to dressing in the tiny shower space, but he pulled his boxers on, not wanting to flaunt anything in front of Adam. He also decided to throw on a T-shirt before heading into the open locker room so Adam wouldn't see his doughboy stomach.

In the locker room, Adam was already tying his shoes. Ru leaned over to kiss him, delving deep, since no one else was around. They stayed that way for a while before Adam's phone pinged. "That will be Mom," he said, pulling away. "Dinner's almost done, I bet." He pulled out the phone, glanced at it, and nodded, flashing it in Ru's direction. "She wants to know if you're coming for dinner."

"As long as I'm invited." Ru pulled his clothes on and bundled up in the giant fluffy jacket Tommy had Binks pick up for him. No one else was wearing anything that thick yet, but Ru was grateful to finally be warm when he went outside and didn't care how ridiculous he looked.

They went home hand in hand, had a great family dinner, and Ru even took out his guitar, strumming through a few cover songs he knew that had Adam's family singing along. Adam's parents left them alone just after nine with the deal that Ru had to leave at eleven. Adam and Ru seemed to be in unspoken agreement that they would make the most of it.

"What do you wanna do?" Adam asked, voice all soft and hesitant when they entered his room and shut the door.

Ru stretched out on Adam's twin bed and patted the spot beside him. When Adam lay down, he turned and wrapped his arm around the younger man's waist, pulling him close, then dove in for a kiss. They stayed that way for a while, lips locked, bodies held gently together. Ru could tell Adam was excited. He was too but wasn't going to push for more just yet. They had time. Adam's touches were tentative, shy, but sweet. Ru returned each gentle touch with one of his own, hands gliding over the bare skin of Adam's stomach, which was beautifully flat and fairly toned. He even let his fingers wander over Adam's taut nipples and then up over his shoulders and down his back to rest on that firm butt he'd been ogling.

Adam never pushed him away, but Ru watched for a rise in tension and pulled back to give him more time whenever they hit that point. There was no rush. If Ru had any say about it, this relationship was going to last for a very, very long time.

CHAPTER 16

THE next three weeks were a whirlwind. Adam quickly became the go-to guy for other students who had questions on something in one of his classes. He spoke up, turned in his homework early, even had people waiting to study with him for final period. Bas protested only a little, until one of the jocks had tried to get up when he sat down, and Adam gave the guy the stink eye until he sat back down. People were talking to Adam in the hallways, like everyone suddenly knew who he was and wanted to be his friend. He just smiled and waved, eager to get on to his next class and then to the final bell, when he could race to the parking lot and find Ru.

He was always there in that same dark town car. They had a few dinners at Dimitri's and a few movies. Ru worked out each night while Adam ran. He had great upper-body strength, and he was improving his own running skills. After a week Ru could run for almost an hour without his legs quaking. Adam worked out with Ru, lifting weights like he had never done before. He'd taken weight training and yoga classes, but nothing interested him as much as running. Ru, however, seemed to feel more at ease when he was lifting.

Ru left town only once during that time, gone for just a day and a half before returning. And each weekend he stayed at Adam's place. Friday he showed up with his bag and guitar and didn't leave until late Sunday night.

They spent a lot of those nights kissing and touching. Adam knew Ru was probably used to going a lot further than he'd gotten, but he felt no pressure from Ru. They both touched each other, exploring in ways that blew Adam's mind. One night they were locked in a deep embrace, and Adam felt pretty good with the pressure of Ru's thigh against his groin.

He didn't realize he was moving his hips against the other man until his whole world seemed to erupt in an embarrassing rush of liquid, heat, and pleasure. Adam ripped himself away and rushed into the bathroom, shocked and a little scared. Sure, he knew the basics but never had expected it to be so sudden, so good, or so embarrassing. His boxers were a mess. All his clean clothes were in the other room with Ru. And Adam was too mortified to open the door. Ru probably thought he was such a kid.

"Adam?" Ru called softly through the door. "It's okay."

No, it really wasn't. His heart was pounding, and he felt like an idiot.

"Adam, baby, let me in please. Let's talk about this. I promise it's okay." When he didn't say anything or open the door, Ru continued, "Do you want me to get your dad?"

"No. God, no!"

"Okay, okay. It's okay. I've got a clean pair of boxers here. If you open the door a little, I can give them to you."

Adam unlocked the door and opened it a crack, staying behind the door. He snatched the boxers from Ru's hand and quickly closed the door, relocking it. He took a fast shower, which eased some of the shakiness. When he finally returned to the bedroom, he was sure his face still burned with embarrassment, but Ru lay on his bed, looking casual, like it was no big deal.

"First time?" Ru asked gently.

Adam nodded, feeling like such a kid. "I know most guys have magazines and stuff. They talk about it in the locker room, but I just never...."

Ru got up from the bed and wrapped his arms around Adam, hugging him tightly. "It's okay. And you know I'm not going to push you. What happened, well, it happens sometimes, even to guys who do it on their own all the time. You know it's okay, right? Did it feel good?"

"Yeah." *Really, really good.* "But I didn't mean to."

Ru kissed him again. "Come lay down with me. It's okay. I'm just gonna hold you."

They got back on the bed, and Adam let himself relax into Ru's arms.

"It's okay to feel good sometimes, you know?"

"Dad says it should be about who it's with and not what I'm doing."

"I agree. Are you okay with that happening with me?"

"Yeah." Adam ran his fingers down Ru's arm. He had really nice arms. "Maybe it wouldn't have been so bad if it wasn't just me. You know, if it was, like, mutual." He flushed again. "Maybe if I hadn't pulled away." *Should he touch Ru? Make him feel good too?*

"Shh." Ru kissed him. "We have plenty of time for that. I'm not going anywhere."

They had several other almost encounters, but Ru often scaled them back while they were both panting and practically begging for more. Adam was feeling more confident about it and not so embarrassed about his first time. He wished he had someone to talk to about it that wasn't Ru or his dad, but didn't trust anyone at school enough to share his little secret.

Halloween came and went, with Ru and Adam dressing up as vampires and handing out candy at Adam's house. Adam's mom made a huge dinner of eggplant parmesan, which had made Ru cringe until Adam goaded him into trying it. When Ru had asked for a second helping, Adam hid a smile. He had a feeling Ru's experience with food that wasn't takeout was limited. Whenever they sat down with snacks, Adam had veggies, and Ru just sort of looked green until they'd found a dip he'd liked, which really was just a light hummus. Everything in Adam's house was homemade, from the pizza dough to the chicken nuggets.

Sometimes Ru would comment on how he had to be packing on the pounds with all the good food he ate, yet Adam didn't see it. In fact, with all of their working out, Ru seemed to be toning up. And Adam was already crazy about Ru's arms and shoulders. The man could have been on display for having such a fine physique. When Ru let out the occasional snarky comment about his weight or his looks, Adam brushed it off, ignoring it instead of acknowledging it. His mom said that the only way for Ru to feel better about himself was to begin seeing himself as he was and not what he thought other people saw. So Adam pointed things out, like the definition in Ru's arms or the firmness of his cute butt, which made the man blush each time.

He hoped it was working. Though he noticed that on Halloween, Ru didn't have a single piece of candy. He did, however, share a caramel apple with Adam. The sticky sweetness had made for interesting kisses, which made Adam smile just at the memory.

The Tuesday of the second week of November, Nate appeared in Adam's study hour, bringing his brain to a screaming halt. Homecoming was that Friday, and Nate so needed to be on the field practicing. "What are you doing here?" Adam asked him as the footballer dropped into the chair beside him.

"You're like the invisible man. You quit football, and everyone talks about you and how great you are, so smart and confident and smiling like a goon the past few weeks, but I never see you. So I figured I'd find you here and see if you want to run today," Nate said, getting up from the chair. Bas walked into the room, pausing when he saw them, then shaking his head and making his way to a group of students gathered in the corner around some French books.

"I run every day. I just don't do it here. Shouldn't you be practicing?"

"Coach gave us all free workout time tonight. So I have to do something, but I'd rather run than play test tackles with Jonah and Hank." He stepped in close, almost inside Adam's personal space. "You were the only true athlete on the team. When you quit, it's all just about who can tackle the most guys. It's so dumb. At least I knew if I threw the ball, you'd be there to catch it."

"And get tackled by the gorillas on the other team 'cause our offensive line could never move fast enough to catch up and guard me." Adam set his book bag on the table and began to line up the homework he had yet to finish for the day.

"I get it. I do. Can I at least run with you? I haven't felt that challenged in weeks."

That meant cutting into Adam's time with Ru, but they never did anything at the gym other than work out anyway. When Adam's folks weren't there, they didn't even hold hands anymore, after one particularly large bodybuilder had called them fags in passing. Adam didn't like the word much and hadn't really heard it outside of media and the books he had been reading about kids his age coming out. It really did get under his skin just thinking about it, being judged so quickly by people who didn't know him at all. Ru didn't seem bothered, but Adam didn't want it directed at either of them again anytime soon.

"Sure. If you want to, meet me at the community center after school. I use their indoor track to run," Adam told him. Now that they were into November, the cold air had really begun to settle in. There was no running outside anymore.

Nate rewarded him with a glowing smile, not his normal, high-school-jock subdued one. "Thanks. I'll see you there." He got up and left while Adam glared at his homework.

"Watch for grabby hands," Bas whispered into his ear a moment later, and then he stalked back to his group.

Ru's smile had been tight when Adam told him about it on their way to the center, but he still took Adam's hand and squeezed. "You really don't talk about him much. Are you even friends?"

"I don't know. We just sort of ran together. I was the running back and sometimes the wide receiver for our football team. Last year he wasn't quarterback, so he would guard me, but even he couldn't keep up. I used to be the best on the team at scoring touchdowns. I mean, they chose me for my ability to haul ass to begin with, and then when he made quarterback, he suggested to the coach this year that we try running more at practice. I thought he was trying to help." Adam picked at the seam of his jeans. "I guess he's a friend. Though we have never hung out or anything."

"But he doesn't know you're gay?"

Adam shook his head. "I don't know if I'm ready for that yet. Some books make it sound so easy, others are really scary."

Ru pulled Adam in for a kiss. "You know my story, right?"

"Picture kissing a boy on a cell phone."

"The first few days, I hid. I was so afraid of seeing anyone and having to witness their disgust.... Then I realized it didn't matter. Those people who were looking at me like that, treating me so bad, it was just 'cause they need to do it to make themselves feel better. Because I've made myself more important than them despite being gay." His warm fingers snuck under Adam's shirt and curled around his side. "And you know what my reward is? You, baby." He smiled. "Adam."

"Somehow I think it would be easier to just be outed."

"I can kiss you in front of him if you want."

"Please don't. I'm crazy about you, but you've seen our football team. They are all frickin' huge."

"And your school has a no-bullying policy," he pointed out.

But Adam just wasn't ready yet. Would Ru hate him if he said so? Adam looked away and glared out the window. The snow had melted, usually did when it came this early. Now everything was just a big muddy mess.

Ru tugged on Adam's hand. "It's okay."

"To not tell anyone yet?"

"Yeah."

"Thanks." Adam glanced his way, and this time the smile reached his eyes.

Nate wasn't there when they arrived, so Ru and Adam headed to the locker room to get changed. Adam's knees were mostly healed. There had even been a little scarring, but thanks to some lotion and the daily workouts, they weren't stiff. When they got upstairs to the track area, Nate sat on one of the benches lifting something that was probably more than Adam's body weight.

"Hey, Nate," Adam called out. The footballer glanced up, put the weight back, and then sat up. Adam motioned to Ru. "This is my friend Ru. Ru, this is Nate." Ru held out his hand, and Nate returned it in the traditional guy clench. Neither of them spoke, but Nate seemed confused. "We usually start with a run to get the blood flowing and then move to weights. Just let me stretch a little first." Adam walked by them to the edge of the track and laid out his towel. Ru joined him for some basic yoga stretches.

"What happened to your knees?" Nate asked, coming up behind them.

"Major wipeout a couple weeks ago." Adam sat on the mat and did a few hip stretches. "You should stretch if you're going to run."

Nate sighed and began doing a few very mild stretches. When Ru and Adam stepped onto the track, he followed. Adam sort of expected Nate to do some sort of sprint like he always had at practice, but he let them set the pace, and Adam always set himself to Ru, who was getting really good at running for longer periods of time.

They ran for just over an hour. Ru's watch beeped, and that meant time to stretch and do some weights. It was the night for shoulders, arms, and chest, so they worked and counted for each other, none of them really talking. Adam felt the tension between the two other guys but didn't get why. Was it just because Ru was a stranger to Nate?

Nate had left the weight room twice, coming back more agitated each time. If this was how the guy was going to act, Adam was going to say they couldn't work out together anymore.

Adam lay back on the bench after checking his weights and waited for Ru to step up and spot him for a chest press. Nate moved up instead. Ru looked briefly irritated but let it go. When it happened on the second set, Adam could see the storm brewing on Ru's face. So he spoke up. "Nate, let Ru spot this time. We've been doing this a while. We've sort of got this partnership thing going." Adam tried to make it sound as neutral as he could.

Nate dropped the weight he'd been on the verge of handing to Adam, forcing Adam to take the brunt of it pretty quickly as it flattened to his chest. Ru was there in half a second to pull it off and then put it back in on the rack. "What the fuck, man?" Ru shouted at Nate. "You could have hurt him!"

"Since you're here I guess he'll be fine. Right, *partner?*"

Adam suddenly felt nauseous. Had he said something wrong? Did Nate know?

"You're the one who butted in. We've been working out for weeks. Something Adam needs to do well in school and stay the happy-go-lucky guy you know him as. So don't be getting up in our faces when you're intruding," Ru snapped back.

"And before you came along, he was running everyday with me."

Was it some sort of contest? Adam was confused. "But I quit football 'cause Hank kept bugging me."

"And where were *you* then, pal?" Ru asked Nate. "When your friend was shoving him into lockers just for running with you?"

"I stopped Hank from hitting him!"

"But not from spreading rumors, which I've heard all about, by the way. It also didn't stop you from bullying other kids, did it? Like Adam's friend, Bas?" They were now inches away from each other, face-to-face, both looking angry enough to kill.

"Hey, guys. Let's calm down a little, okay?" Adam tried.

"I am fucking calm. I *see* what's been going on with you," Nate said. "Do you?" He fished his phone out of his pocket and began looking for something on the screen. "You know, I saw you with him a couple of weeks ago, coming out of the bargain theater. I thought it was weird, that maybe it wasn't really you. But it was, wasn't it?"

Adam felt his stomach flip over.

"Don't you recognize this guy? He's all over MTV and VH1. Ryunoski Nakimura, kicked out of Vocal Growth for being a pervert. I thought all you boy-band types were fags anyway. So you're here doing what, trying to get into Adam's pants? He's straight, you know, not your type. Go back to faggotland."

Ru reacted before the words could sink in for Adam by smashing his fist into Nate's face. Blood burst from Nate's nose like a ripe melon exploding. Adam should have moved, done something. Nate didn't try to retaliate; he was too blinded by pain and shock. Ru looked at his fist, as if unsure of what he'd just done.

"Look it up, Adam. All you have to do is Google his name," Nate grumbled, sounding funny since his nose was pouring blood. He ripped a towel off the rack and stuck it to his nose. "He's going to be hosting the fucking Diva awards. What kind of guy does that?"

Adam glanced at Ru, who wouldn't look at him. "And your point to all this, Nate?" Adam finally asked. "If Ru is who you say he is, even if he's gay, why does it matter? Why all the in-your-face crap? What did he do to you?"

Nate held up his phone, showing Adam a picture. The photo was of Ru locked in a very intimate embrace with another guy. The kiss looked pretty deep. "How about what he's doing to you? Do you know he's with this other guy?"

"I'm not," Ru protested.

But Nate continued, "Did you know he's all over the news hanging off his bandmate, Tommy Foster? The media says they're lovers, him and a bunch of other guys. Apparently this guy gets around. And now he's pretending to be what, your workout buddy? I hate fakers."

Adam's world swirled around him a minute or two. He could hardly process the words Nate said because he was still focused on that picture. His head throbbed, and his gut churned, not with fear but with jealousy. Was Ru seeing someone else? Sure, Adam knew he'd been with other guys before. Was this an old flame? The one who'd outed him, maybe? And why did it hurt so much to actually see it? Finally Adam decided he needed to put an end to their bickering before it got out of hand. He realized then that he really didn't care what Nate thought, because as Ru had said before, Nate wasn't one of those people who mattered in Adam's life.

"Well, I pretty much hate idiots, but we are all that sometimes. Do you hate fags too? Think they are all whores and believe whatever the media tells you?" Adam couldn't believe the word came from his mouth. It tasted bad when he said it.

"Why? What does it matter?" Nate said. "You have a right to know that the guy you're working out with is checking you out. He might even attack you in the locker room!"

"Do you hate fags?" Adam demanded.

Nate glared at him, refusing to answer.

"You can go. I won't be running with you anymore since I'm one of those things you hate so much." When the words left his mouth, Adam suddenly felt freed. Like the repercussions didn't matter. It just felt good to tell someone. Even if everyone found out. He was so tired of hiding who he was. Tired of being afraid of what others thought. Others he cared nothing at all for.

Nate's eyes almost bugged out of his head. "You're telling me you're gay."

Adam sighed. "Bye, Nate." He left the workout area, his mind spinning so fast he was dizzy. He showered and changed on autopilot and then sat down on the bench. He texted his dad, asking for a ride, not sure about all the things in his head about Ru. It had to be an old picture. Probably *the* picture that Ru said had outed him. Outed him to the world. *Crap.* Ru really was famous. A celebrity. Why hadn't he said anything? Didn't he trust Adam?

Ru's hand landed on his shoulder. "Can we talk?"

"Is what he said the truth?"

"About what? Who I am, or all the guys the media says I'm screwing?"

Adam folded his arms around his head, an odd rush of tears coming to his eyes. He fought to keep them from falling. "Why wouldn't you tell me? I mean, it makes sense. You sing nice and play the guitar really well. And since you're always working weird hours and stuff.... I just thought you trusted me."

"I do."

"Then why not tell me?"

"It's not easy for a lot of people to take. And after what happened with Kris, I'm a little more cautious."

"Distrustful," Adam clarified.

"It doesn't change anything," Ru insisted. "I'm still crazy about you. I'm still the guy you've been hanging out with for the past couple weeks. The stuff in the magazines and TV, that's all for show. The hair, the makeup. You have to understand that."

"I don't know." Adam needed to talk to someone, his dad, his mom, someone not Ru. "Can I talk with you tomorrow? Can I just have the night to sort it all out?" Adam couldn't look at him; he'd break if he did.

"Okay," Ru whispered, hurt in his voice. "Let me take you home."

Adam waved him away. "My dad's on the way."

The silence was so long Adam almost looked up, but he knew what he'd see on Ru's face: the worry, the hurt, the fear. He hated putting it there, but he needed time to think.

"Promise me you'll talk to me before you make assumptions," Ru finally said.

"I will. I promise. I just need to talk to my parents. I just need a little bit of time to process everything. And I think I just came out." He was pretty sure Nate would be off telling everyone he was gay and that it would be the buzz of the school by tomorrow morning.

"Okay. Is it all right if I wait until your dad gets here? I just wanna make sure you get home safe."

Adam nodded. They sat in silence until his dad appeared. The man shot a questioning look at Ru but led Adam out of the building and into the car without asking a thing. Adam waited until the car headed toward home before letting the tears ago.

When he could talk, he told his dad everything. It felt good to let it all out, and it didn't hurt as much once he'd put it all on the table. None of it was life ending. He didn't really believe that Ru was cheating on him. And finding out his boyfriend was famous wasn't the worst thing that could have happened to him, though he was unsure of what it meant for them as a couple.

His father, as usual, was very rational. "I can certainly understand him not walking up to you and saying 'Hey, I'm famous, wanna go out with me?'"

Adam laughed lightly as they made their way into the house. The smell of cookies baking hit him and made his stomach flip in a happy dance. How many times had his mother made those awesome cookies to pull him out of some weird funk? How had she known? He smiled at her as he sat down at the kitchen counter. His dad filled her in on the events of the day. She just nodded, then took another batch out of the oven.

While Adam munched on a handful of cookies, she played with her iPad, finally pausing to turn it his way. "Is this the picture Nate showed you?" She held up an enlarged picture of Ru kissing the other guy.

Adam flinched. "Yeah."

"Ex-boyfriend," his mom said. "Kris Turlington, it says. Apparently the guy was cheating on Ru with a half-dozen other guys. The picture is from over seven months ago." She navigated to another screen. There were pictures of a smiling Ru with an older guy, both glammed up like the picture that Ru had sent Adam late one night. "The other guy in this picture is Tommy Foster, former bandmate to Ru. They are supposed to be really good friends. This picture was about two weeks ago. There are a lot of rumors about them being a couple, but both deny it." Tommy had his arm around Ru's shoulders, and they looked comfortable together. The picture showed a level of intimacy that made Adam jealous.

"Do you think he and Tommy are together?" Adam whispered.

"I think we raised you better than to believe in rumors," his mom said. The doorbell rang. His dad got up and headed to answer it. Adam feared it might be Ru, or worse, Nate. A minute later, it was Bas who walked into the kitchen with his dad.

"Bas?"

He sat down at the counter and waved Adam's parents away. They left the room, his mom turning off the oven as she went. She patted Adam's hand and gave him a sympathetic look. His heart lurched into his throat.

"What are you doing here?"

"Nate's already spreading the word. I thought you should know," Bas said quietly.

Adam glared at the countertop refusing to meet his eyes, not for shame at what he was, but because he'd been revealed to be a coward. "I'm sorry I never stood up for you."

Bas took his hand. "Honey, you always stand up for me. Ever since that day you found me in the bathroom with my pants around my ankles, bleeding from a major head wound. I would never have been able to return to Northern if it weren't for you. I could walk through the halls and even sit with you at lunch and no one would bother me. Sure, people aren't always nice, but that's not your fault."

Adam looked at him and sighed. They'd grown up together. Known each other all through junior high on up but had never really been close. Adam really never let anyone close because he always felt so different. Was that part of being gay? Just never feeling like he had a place. "So the whole school will know by tomorrow morning."

"Probably. I'm sorry."

"What about Ru?"

Bas looked confused. "Who's Ru?"

"My boyfriend. Didn't Nate saying anything about that?"

"No. But boy, you better spill. You have a boyfriend? Was this the hot guy you met in the library?"

Adam frowned at Bas. "Did you know?"

"That you're gay?" He shrugged. "I suspected, especially after your careful change of the pronouns, but we gay boys don't out each other. There's a lot more queers on campus than what you think, that's for sure."

"None of it mattered until I met Ru. I was just going to finish high school and then move to some state where no one cares...." He put his hands in his hair and tugged, something Ru usually did when he was frustrated. Adam was so jealous, of Kris, of Tommy, of anyone who had Ru. How would it be possible to share Ru with the whole world? The guy was famous; that meant people everywhere wanted a piece of him. "I don't know what to do."

"About what? Nate? That genie is out of the bottle, sweetie. Pretty much no putting it back in at this point."

"About Ru. He hid things from me."

"Well, I hate to break in with news of the real world, sunshine, but we all hide things from people, especially the people we want most to impress. We fear that if we show it all, let it all hang out, that they won't want us. So unless he's hiding a major drug habit or a half-devoured Siamese twin, I think you'll get over it." Bas sat back in the chair and took a cookie. "Be grateful you have parents who are okay with you being you. And a boyfriend who's not afraid to hold your hand in public."

"I thought your parents were okay," Adam said, trying to think back to the times in junior high when he'd seen Bas' folks.

Bas shook his head. "Nope. I live with my grandma now. Mom and Dad had a huge fight after I came out. Dad wanted to send me to one of those places that reprogram gays. Mom wanted nothing to do with me. They divorced, but neither of them wanted me. Grandma took me in."

Adam grabbed his hand. "I'm so sorry."

"Not your fault. Not mine either. It's hard sometimes to believe that it's not my fault. But it really isn't. If they'd loved each other, or even me, they'd have worked it out."

"Ru's family was like that. His dad walked out of his life when he was eleven. He's been alone so long."

Bas squeezed Adam's hand. "Well, he's not alone anymore, is he?"

Adam shook his head.

"So tell me about this boyfriend of yours. Is he hot?"

"He's a rock star," Adam said. The words leaving him felt a lot like they should have been whispered.

"Of course. First loves are always like rock stars."

"No. I mean, really. He's a rock star. Like famous and all that."

"For real?"

Adam pulled out his phone and surfed to the pictures he'd taken of Ru sleeping. "I guess he doesn't look like this when he goes out and sings and stuff, but here he is, Ryunoski Nakimura."

"Wait, like the former Vocal Growth band member, Ryunoski Nakimura?" Bas grabbed the phone and stared at the picture. "Damn, boy, you don't do anything halfway, do you? Okay, details. I need details. How did all this happen, and why haven't you said anything sooner?"

So Adam laid it all out on the line, happy for once to be able to speak to someone his own age about his relationship troubles. Maybe Bas could share some insights that he hadn't thought of yet.

CHAPTER 17

WHEN Ru stepped into the condo, the utter stillness of it smashed into him like a two-ton bag of depression falling from the ceiling and hitting him dead center in the soul. Adam had been so quiet, so still, and so hurt that Ru wasn't sure how to fix it. He should have told him sooner. He knew that. He'd just been too afraid. And now he'd made a fool of himself and forced Adam to out himself to the most popular guy in school.

Ru sunk down onto the couch and yanked at his hair. He was as bad as Kris. This whole thing felt like a duplicate of his ex-boyfriend's betrayal, only it was he who had done it to Adam. Lying, hiding, and finally flipping out. But Nate had kept pushing his way in closer, brushing against Adam when they were working out. Ru knew Adam didn't notice. The guy was oblivious to a lot of the open sexual aggression of the world. He never noticed when someone smiled at him or let a caress linger too long. He was an eager lover, but an inexperienced one who didn't know how to ward off a forceful guy like Nate.

Ru picked up his guitar and began to strum. He paused long enough to turn on a digital recorder as he ran through angry chords and a mash of hurt-dripping words. He was just venting, needing to get out all the swirls of fear and pain in his head. The door opened, and Tommy walked in looking tired, but Ru didn't stop. He let out all his frustrations and hoped he would have something he could salvage from it later when his head was calm enough to think.

Tommy disappeared into his room, only to return and perch on the edge of the sofa a minute later. When Ru finally ran out of steam, they both let silence run through the room for a few minutes. Finally Tommy spoke. "Gonna call that one 'A Sailor's Tale'? I don't think I've ever heard you swear so much."

Ru sighed. He had the odd urge to smash something. Too bad he didn't have Nate's face still within reach. His fist hurt from the punch, and he'd been shocked it had happened. He had never hit anyone in his life, and that had just come up like a reflex. It was probably all over the news already. *Former Boy Band Star Attacks High School Student.* "Long night."

"Things okay with Adam? I thought you'd be with him."

"I was. But he found out that I'm not Ru, but Ryunoski Nakimura, pariah of the whole Western world."

Tommy sighed. "By 'found out,' I assume you mean you didn't tell him, but he found out in some roundabout way. You're still Ru, even when you're a dumbass. I think he'll figure that out pretty fast." He took the guitar and set it aside, then clicked off the digital recorder. "So what happened, and why is there blood on your clothes?"

Ru glanced down, realizing he hadn't changed. He probably stank too, since he'd been running like mad and that made him sweat. "I hit him."

"Adam?" Tommy asked, alarmed.

"No, Nate, the guy who was hanging all over Adam. He almost hurt Adam by dropping a weight on him, and then he insulted me, and it just happened." Ru looked at his hand, flexing it, staring at the dried blood on it. "It was all so fast."

"Okay, let's get you cleaned up. Then you're going to tell me really slow what happened." Tommy pulled Ru up and shoved him into the bathroom. He turned on the hot water and left him with, "You have ten minutes before I'm coming in to get your ass. So hurry up."

Ru was out in five. He pulled on a pair of sleep pants and nothing else. His whole body hurt, and he didn't think it was from the workouts. He'd begun to enjoy them, not only because he was spending time with Adam, but because it made him less tired and his body seemed to feel really good after being pushed hard.

"You been eating?" Tommy asked when Ru dumped himself on a huge cushion beside the couch.

"Yeah, three square and a couple snacks. Protein shake after weight lifting if Adam's mom doesn't cook." Which was rare. Ru's stomach made a growling noise. He hadn't eaten yet. He'd been too worried about Adam's reaction to think about food until now. He got up and went to the kitchen to throw together a protein shake. The chocolate-peanut butter-banana mix tasted really good. He sat back down on his pillow with the shake. "Do I look like I've gained weight? 'Cause I feel like I've really been killing it in the gym."

"Nope. You look fine." Tommy was still looking at him.

"What?" Ru demanded.

"You're talking about protein shakes and weight lifting like you enjoy it. You, the guy who hates bending over to tie his shoes."

"Shoes should slip on," Ru stated. "But yeah. I've been working out with Adam. Running every day for like an hour, then another hour of weight lifting. On the weekends it's longer, and then we go do something fun. Like last weekend we went rollerblading, which by the way, I'm awful at."

"Okay. So explain what happened tonight and why I came home to sailor-mouthed Ru."

So Ru told him the whole story.

"But you're going to call him, right? Or at least text him. Adam needs to know those pictures were old—well, the one of Kris. And if you want, I can talk to him to assure him that I'm not banging you." Tommy kicked off his shoes.

"As if."

"What? You're not bangable?"

"I am bangable—just, you and me in that way? Um, weird and kinda gross."

"Thanks, man. Love you too." Tommy got up and started taking off layers. He must have come from a shoot because he had on coats and multiple shirts. "I think I stay in Diego too much, 'cause it is frickin' cold out there."

Ru leaned against the back of the couch, sucking on the last of his shake. He should get up and have a salad to get some vitamins in too, but he was probably going to call it an early night. Without Adam, he didn't think he could find the motivation to do much more for the day. He wondered what the blond was doing.

"Call him."

Ru glanced up and threw Tommy an annoyed look.

"Don't look at me like that. Every time you get that goofy look on your face, you're thinking about him. Have you even played the song for him? You know, the one you wrote about him?"

Ru shook his head, not wanting to think about it. "He told me he wanted time. I'm just respecting his wishes."

"You were already a dumbass for not telling him sooner, but don't be a dumbass and let him stew on this. Call him. Tell him you're sorry. Play 'Start Something' for him. If you want to keep him, that is. If he doesn't wind up in your arms in a blubbery mess by the end of the song, he's not the right guy for you."

"I can't live without him."

"Ru...."

"I'm serious, Tommy. The past couple weeks have been the best of my life. I feel in tune with the music, with my body, my soul, my heart, and Adam. If I can't have him, I will fall apart. I can't go through what I did with Kris again. I lived in this void of feeling for six months. Like nothing could touch me unless I let it. I wrapped myself in iron and avoided the whole world. I can't go back to that. If Adam doesn't want me...."

Tommy crossed the room and wrapped his arms around Ru, hugging him tight. "Don't talk like that, kiddo. I need you around. So let's work this out, okay?"

The door clicked again, and Binks held it open. Both Tommy and Ru looked up as Adam walked in with a guy neither of them knew. Binks nodded to them and backed out, closing the door behind them. Adam blinked at them, as if shocked, but then Ru realized he hadn't put a shirt on, and Tommy was hugging him, so it looked like more than it was.

Ru pulled away and wiped his tears away with the back of his hand. The unknown guy gripped Adam's arm to keep him from bolting. Tommy recovered first, getting up and striding across the room, hand outstretched to shake Adam's hand.

"You must be Adam. It's good to finally meet you. I'm Tommy."

Adam took his hand, but his face was one big question.

Tommy yanked Adam into a hug. "Be good to him, okay?" he said quietly. "He's like my kid brother, and he's terrified you're gonna break his heart. Please don't."

Adam nodded as Tommy let go. "Um, this is my friend Sebastian." He motioned to the unknown guy. "He sort of talked me into coming. Helped me work out some of the stuff in my head."

So this was the guy that Adam wrote about. The one Ru had written a song about. Ru got up, suddenly feeling very naked without his shirt. "Sorry, I just got out of the shower. Let me grab a shirt." He darted off toward his room.

"Don't cover up on my account, sweetie," Sebastian called after him.

Ru pulled a shirt over his head and made his way back to the living room. Adam still stood as though rooted to the same spot, but Bas was off talking to Tommy about some of the different guitars and art that hung on the walls. They were probably trying to give them a sense of privacy. Ru walked over to Adam and suddenly wished he had pockets in his pajama pants because he wanted really badly to pull Adam into his arms or at least touch him but knew it probably wasn't a good idea. "Hey."

"Hey," Adam replied.

"I'm glad you came over. I wanted to say I'm sorry. For not telling you sooner. It was a stupid thing to do. I really wanted to tell you. I was scared you'd freak out and leave me."

"It's okay. I understand. I probably wouldn't have believed you. Probably would have been too afraid to send that first text."

Ru smiled. "Yeah, about me liking Madonna."

Adam flushed, and it was so hot that Ru wanted to drag him into his bedroom so they could just hold each other while the rest of the world worked out whatever it needed to. "Sorry about that."

"No reason to be. I do like Madonna."

Adam took a step closer, like he was asking to be touched without saying the words. Ru reached out and pulled him into his arms. He rested his cheek against Adam's and was just grateful to have his warmth back. "Please forgive me, Adam."

"Nothing to forgive," Adam said. "I was just so jealous, seeing you with someone else. It was awful, like someone hit me in the gut and then reached up to yank out my heart. I've never felt like that before."

"But that's all in the past. Kris was ages ago, and he messed me up." Ru glanced over at Tommy, who was engaged in a conversation about electronic keyboards with Bas. "Tommy is my family. He's the only one who has ever been okay with me."

Adam squeezed Ru hard. "My family is yours now too."

"Even though you had to out yourself for me?"

Adam pulled back enough so they could stare each other in the eyes. "That was like a weight lifted off my shoulders. Bas came over 'cause he got a call from one of the computer kids, who is the younger brother of one of the jockstraps, who found out from Nate. The whole school will know by tomorrow."

"I'm sorry."

Adam shrugged. "Whatever happens happens for a reason." He waved at Bas. "He suspected. I've been a bad friend. Kept him away. We were friends in junior high, until I started realizing that I liked guys. He also encouraged me to come here, even drove, and you know parking around here sucks."

Ru smiled. "Wouldn't know. Binks does all that for me."

"Totally makes sense why you have your own private driver, you being famous and all."

"He's bodyguard-trained too, but I haven't had any issues here yet. Well, until word gets out from Nate that I'm here."

"That's the weird thing," Adam said. "Nate didn't pass on anything about you being here. He just told Jonah that I admitted to being gay, and that's why I left the football team. Which is a total lie. I left 'cause I hated football." He looked at Sebastian and Tommy. "I think I just realized today that I really don't have any friends at school except maybe Bas. I mean, I never trusted anyone. I was afraid they'd know I was different if I got too close. So really, I have no right to be mad at you. And maybe now that it's out in the open, I can start over."

"I wish I could be there with you at school."

Adam laughed. "Apparently you're a big deal, so you'd have girls chasing you everywhere and all the guys wanting to kick your ass 'cause their girl looked your way." He sobered a little. "What about the media? I mean, are they gonna start pounding on my door?"

Ru shrugged. "I really don't know. With Kris they did, but he was in Diego with me, and he wanted the spotlight, so he would call and tip them off as to where we'd be. It took me ages and our breakup to figure out why the paps could always find us. You said that Nate wasn't saying anything about me being here. Maybe that's a good thing. It will give us time to spin it, keep the paps away. I'll call Katie—she's my manager—and get her take on it."

"It must be horrible having to live in the lights all the time, everything you do recorded and then analyzed twenty different ways." Adam reached out and grabbed Ru's hand.

"The fame is nice sometimes but mostly just lonely. It's hard to know who to trust. Even harder to let someone get close. Guess you and me have that in common." Ru glanced at Bas and Tommy. "It's late, but how about we sit down for a civilized meal? There's a Thai place around the corner that has the most amazing lettuce wraps."

Adam tugged at Ru's oversized T-shirt. "You gonna get dressed, then? Or we hiding out now?"

"I'll get dressed." Ru glanced at the bag Adam had dropped just inside the doorway. He hadn't noticed it before, but it looked like his overstuffed book bag.

Adam followed his line of sight and smiled. "My stuff for school tomorrow and some clothes. Mom and Dad said it's okay if I spend the night as long as you can get me to school on time tomorrow." His cheeks burned bright red. "They gave me a little 'care package' too, but I haven't opened it."

Ru had no idea what to say, so instead he pulled Adam into a kiss deep enough to leave them both wanting. It was Tommy who interrupted them. "Whoa, whoa, whoa! We've got a guest, boys!"

Adam's flush was sweet, but Ru winked at Tommy. "Let's go get some food, and then Adam and I can continue this later."

"Okay, okay. I can take a hint. Get dressed, sailor boy."

Dinner at the little Thai place was good. Ru found having Tommy, Bas, and Adam with him made for light conversation and a good selection of foods, since they all ordered something different and were willing to share. He spent the entire time sitting next to Adam, their hands nestled firmly together, laughing and sharing an occasional kiss. They joked about California weather and the Minnesota snow. Bas never once asked for an autograph, though he did confess to being a Vocal Growth fan. No one bothered them, paps didn't show up, and other than Tommy's phone ringing once, no one interrupted. He wondered if being with friends was supposed to be like this all the time. No one looked to him at the end of the night to pay. Instead, everyone ponied up a share, and then they boxed up the leftovers and walked back to the condo in relative quiet.

"I'm gonna walk Bas to his car," Tommy said as he bumped shoulders with Ru. "Probably going to spend some time in the studio tonight."

Ru nodded, knowing he was just planning on giving him and Adam some time alone. The idea made him nervous and excited all at once. They made their way upstairs, Adam waving good night to Bas, and Tommy smiling like a goon. When they'd finally stripped out of their winter clothes and made their way to Ru's bedroom, he was sure his heart was pounding. He closed the door, locking it.

He picked up his favorite acoustic, glad Tommy had put it back where it belonged, and sat down on the edge of the bed. "Can I sing for you?"

"Sure," Adam said.

Ru motioned him to sit in the giant Papasan chair. Once Adam had made himself comfortable, Ru began to strum out the soft chords of "Start Something." Even though he didn't have Tommy singing harmony or the sweet sound of the piano, he poured his soul into the song. He met Adam's stunned gaze and sang as though he were performing for millions. When the final notes played, he quieted the strings and closed his eyes to give himself a moment for composure. If he looked at Adam right then, he'd cry, and the last thing he wanted was to be a big baby in front of the guy he was crazy about.

"That was beautiful." Adam was suddenly there, sitting beside him.

Ru set the guitar aside. "I wrote that after our first date."

"You wrote that for me?"

"Yeah." Ru pulled him close and kissed his lips.

"Ready to start something to last forever?" Adam asked when they finally broke the kiss.

"God, I hope so."

Adam pulled him up off the bed. They kissed for a while, just hands together, mouths tasting one another, breathing the shared space.

"We don't have to do anything," Ru said. But Adam had other plans. The younger man pressed their bodies together so tightly Ru couldn't help but notice how excited Adam was. He pulled back a minute to search Adam's face for any sign of reluctance. "Are you sure?"

Adam tugged on Ru's hand, leading him to the bed. "I want to be with you."

"You are with me," Ru assured him.

Adam blushed. "So come kiss me. I want to touch you. Make you happy."

Ru let himself be tugged down onto the bed and rolled over to lie next to Adam. He pressed their hips together, hating the way all the clothes felt between them. "I don't want to rush you."

"You're not. I'm not sure how far I can go. But I want to be with you. I want us to feel good together." Adam ducked his head down, hiding his face in Ru's shoulder. "You know, like *that*."

"Even though it's messy and embarrassing?"

"Even though. 'Cause it's with you."

Ru rubbed Adam's chest. He gave in to the desire to have skin to skin by sitting up and yanking off his shirt. He grabbed at Adam's also until the young man got the hint and pulled off his top, letting it fall to the side of the bed. "Okay. But if you feel weird at all, you say 'elephant,' 'kay?"

"Elephant?" Adam laughed.

"Yeah. How often are you going to say elephant while in bed with someone? You feel weird, or just want to slow down, let me know, 'kay?"

"'Kay." But Adam didn't use the word even once.

CHAPTER 18

ADAM loved waking up beside Ru, though Ru was a bit of a bear in the morning. He'd groaned and grumbled while Adam had gotten up, showered, and made himself presentable for the school day. They hadn't used the care package his parents had left for him, which was, embarrassingly enough, a box of condoms and a bottle of lube. Adam wasn't sure of all the details as to how they were used, but he wasn't going to ask either. He'd just stuffed them into his bag and gotten into the car.

Though Ru had been reluctant to get up, he did accompany Adam to school. In his pajamas, which made Adam laugh. Before Adam got out of the car, Ru rewarded him with a kiss and promised to be waiting for him after school.

Despite the events of yesterday, Adam was hopeful. Maybe school wouldn't be so bad. He made his way inside, praying quietly that maybe, just maybe, the storm would pass with little to no rain. By the time he reached his locker, he knew there would be no such luck. His locker was covered in pink paint, the words unmistakable: fag, faggot, perv, fairy. Adam sighed.

Bas appeared a minute later with a slew of teachers and the principal. Adam blinked at him as they all headed to his locker. Principal O'Brien frowned at the mess but turned Adam's way. "What's your combination, Corbin?"

"Um, 12, 34, 18, 9," Adam told him.

O'Brien opened his locker and began pulling books out. Slips of paper fell around their feet. Notes. Adam gulped. He'd been out less than twenty-four hours, and he was already getting hate mail slipped into his locker? "Am I going somewhere?" he finally asked, since the teachers were holding his books.

"Your locker is being moved next to Axelrod's, which is right next to the teacher's lounge and has cameras on it 24/7. So anyone else who would like to *vandalize school property*," O'Brien said, glaring at the students who were gathered in the hallway, "will get the full penalty, which is expulsion."

Everyone suddenly seemed very interested in getting to class. Adam followed O'Brien to his new locker and got the combination before getting help to rearrange everything. He even got a tardy pass for his first class. Principal O'Brien walked him to that class through empty hallways. "Now, Corbin, I don't want you to think that you're going to get any special privileges."

"I wouldn't expect any, sir. I've been gay my whole life. The only thing different is that everyone knows."

"Northern has a no-tolerance policy when it comes to bullying. Anyone slips you a note or says something to you on the way to the bathroom, you come to me."

Adam blinked at him. "Does it happen to Bas a lot?"

O'Brien frowned. "Unfortunately, yes. Now I assume you've spoken with your parents about this?"

"You mean about me being gay?"

"Yes."

"I have."

"Good. Now I recommend if you need to use the restroom, use the one near the faculty lounge. Not all of the kids care if they graduate or not." With that, he left, and Adam wondered just how much help they would really be if something happened. He sucked in a deep breath and made his way into class. Once he handed off his tardy pass to the teacher, he sat in an open seat, quickly assessing it to make sure it hadn't been tampered with. He could already feel the eyes on him and suspected it would only get worse as the day went on.

By lunchtime Adam was about ready to walk out. Only running into Bas' smiling face and, a few minutes later, an encouraging text from Ru kept him from just sitting down in the corner to cry. He'd had things thrown at him, mostly paper and insults. He'd been shoved into the lockers more times than he could count and even had one of his teachers ignore him completely in class.

He didn't even try to sit at his normal table with Nate and the mash of other random jocks. Instead he found a place in the corner, so he could have his back to the wall and keep an eye out for anyone who approached. Bas chattered away next to him like all was normal with the world.

"Don't let them get to you, sweetie," Bas said.

But every time Adam looked up, he caught people staring and pointing. How awful. He'd never felt so exposed or inadequate. Why did it matter to them? Nothing about him had changed from yesterday when they were all smiling and greeting him like he was their friend.

After choking down half his sandwich, he couldn't take it anymore. He bolted from the table and made his way outside and around to the parking lot to dial a familiar number.

"Aren't you supposed to be in class?" Ru asked when he picked up the phone.

"On lunch break" was all Adam could say. He missed the sound of Ru's voice so much.

"How is it? Are they treating you bad?"

Adam had to breathe deeply for a minute or so before he could answer without bursting into the tears he was fighting. "Yeah."

"I'd come get you, but I think your parents would get mad."

"It's okay. Just talk to me, please. Just until lunch is over and I have to go back."

"Okay. Um, let me tell you a little about how the recording process works. Maybe this weekend I'll bring you down to the studio and give you a tour." Ru rattled on about equipment and processes Adam would probably never keep straight. It really didn't matter what he said, just that he was there, so close and somehow reachable, even though he was so far away.

"Hey, so I gotta go to San Diego tomorrow night. Should be back early Saturday, though. You gonna be okay while I'm gone?"

Adam was on his way to his new locker when the words jolted him out of his zombie-like funk. Ru would be gone only a day and a half, really, but Adam wondered if he'd go nuts by then. "You have to?"

"Yeah, gotta meet with my producer and have a couple interviews. Maybe we can talk your parents into letting you come with me? You'd only miss a day of school."

But even before Adam asked, he knew what his parents would say. Missing school was not an option. "I'll be okay."

"You still want me to pick you up after school?"

"Yes. I need to run. Like forever. And kiss you."

"Okay, baby." It sounded like Ru smiled. "Adam, you're gonna get through this."

"I hope you're right." Adam imagined the rest of his day as people passed him in the busy hallway, and he wondered how long this would last. They'd have to get bored and move on eventually, right?

"I know I'm right. Now don't you have French or something? Get going. See you in a few hours. *Je t'aime.*" Ru said.

Adam let him go with that final French "I love you" and made his way to class. At least the day was almost done. Unfortunately, Nate cornered him in study hall. But Adam had no patience for him at all. "Haven't you done enough, Nate? I thought I told you to stay away from me."

Bas watched from across the room, a huge question on his face.

Nate seemed agitated. "Can I talk to you alone?"

"No." Adam set out his assignments for the day, happy all he had were a few math problems. He was pretty sure he didn't have the focus right now to do anything more intense.

Nate sat down in the chair next to him. "I'm sorry."

"For telling the world I'm gay or for being an asshole to Ru?"

"Look, that guy just isn't good news."

Adam threw him a glare. "Continue that conversation and I'm leaving."

Nate sighed. "I just came to say I'm sorry. I didn't think Jonah was going to go and tell everyone. I just needed someone to talk to. If anyone's bugging you, let me know."

"Why?" Adam asked. "Why do you care? It's not like we were ever friends. You just wanted to use me to help you get a scholarship. The rest of your dopey friends just wanted to smash my face in. Not really stuff that endears."

"I thought we were friends. I was hoping you'd come to the homecoming game."

"I'm sure I have something else to do." Though he really didn't, since Ru was going to be out of town. But Adam would rather sit home alone than get teased at the Homecoming game.

"Please. You may think we were never friends, but you were the only guy who's ever been real to me. You don't look at me and tell me I'm great. You told me I sucked at running. You laughed in my face when I said we'd go to State. No one else has those kind of balls. It was nice not to be lied to."

Adam frowned at Nate. Was his popularity all that different from Ru's? Probably not, other than sheer scale. "I'll think about it."

Nate smiled. "Thank you. That's great. I promise no one will bug you at the game if you come. I'll even talk to the coach about having you sit on the bench. You can shout at me that I suck if I fumble or something."

"I haven't said I'd go yet."

Nate gripped his hand and leaned in close enough to whisper. "I didn't tell anyone that you were with that celebrity guy."

Adam blinked at him a few times, trying to understand his meaning. "You're saying if I don't go, you're going to tell everyone that Ru is here?"

"I'm sure the media would have a field day with that. Probably have a couple hundred pounding on your door for interviews. Maybe some crazy fans too."

"I say we're not friends and you blackmail me?"

Nate shrugged as he got up from his chair. "Think about it. I know you'll make the right choice. See you later." He left the room and everyone seemed to be staring.

"Show's over, kiddies!" Bas shouted at them all. "Either get your asses studying or go the fuck home." He sat down in Nate's vacated chair. "How you holding up?"

"What was that?" Adam asked.

Bas shook his head. "I dunno, sweetie, but don't go anywhere alone."

Adam sighed. He wished he could just skip school and spend a few days with Ru. San Diego was probably pretty warm and sunny this time of year. And anywhere Ru was had to be better than here. "If I go, will you go with me?"

Bas shrugged. "Sure. We can be the homo parade." Adam threw him a dirty look. "Kidding, kidding. So let's talk about the homecoming dance. Are you going to bring Ru?"

"What? No. I'm not going to the dance. I may go to the game, but Ru's not even going to be in town on Friday, so I'm definitely not going to the dance."

"If he were here, would you?"

Adam thought about it. He would love to dance with Ru. He'd love to be that open with him in public, show everyone the amazing guy he'd fallen in love with. But it would be bad. People would recognize Ru. Some might even get violent with them just for being out.

"No." Protecting Ru was the most important thing he could do right now. Even if that meant keeping their relationship a secret. He wasn't going to use Ru to gain popularity or fame like the man's ex had. And he'd play Nate's game if he had to.

THAT night when Ru left, Adam almost fell apart. His parents were there to comfort him when he cried and assure him it would only be a few days. They texted each other right up until Ru had to turn his phone off for the flight. *Call when you land,* Adam texted him.

Promise was Ru's reply.

The school day on Friday was no better than the day before. When he opened his new locker, there were a half-dozen notes that had been stuck in the slots. Adam knew he should bring them to the principal but didn't want to play victim anymore. If he could tell who wrote it, he'd confront them. But he didn't try to open any of them until lunch. Since he'd been eating alone, or with Bas, he figured it didn't matter where he ate. He often called Ru on lunch, but when Adam dialed him today, he was met with Ru's voice mail. The singer was probably in an interview or something.

Adam sucked in a deep breath and opened the first note. The first few were so badly spelled and filled with hate that Adam was positive they came from Hank or Jonah. Neither of whom he wanted to start a brawl with, so he'd give those to the principal. A few others had long rants with biblical quotes. Did they know Adam had excelled in biblical studies? He knew all the quotes, including the ones they didn't think to mention about not shaving or eating certain things on Sundays, all which were as damning as "laying with another man as he would a woman."

Did it even count if they hadn't done that? Adam shook his head and cast the note aside, wondering who the idiot was. He yanked out his laptop and blogged for a couple of minutes, clearing his head by writing from memory the whole section of Deuteronomy, which laid out rules for people a couple thousand years ago to survive. Once he'd gotten most of his ranting out on the computer, he returned to the pile of notes. One was actually encouraging.

Adam,

I wanted to tell you how inspiring you are to me. I've been hiding who I am for years, afraid of what others would do, watching the things they do to Sebastian Axelrod, and he's really not all that different. The fact that you're unwilling to hide any longer gives me strength. See, I was born a girl, but I've never felt like one. I hope to one day find the courage to show people the person I'm supposed to be, not the one that gender demands I be. So no matter what people say or do to you, know you're not alone. We are all afraid. We are all different. That's easy to forget. And these last days of school are just a drop in the bucket of our lives. Don't change yourself to suit them. Maybe someday soon I'll have the strength to do that as well.

It was signed "Mike." Adam wondered who Mike might be. But it wasn't the only encouraging note. There were two others, both from people who claimed to be bullied often, but were inspired by Adam standing up to them. Odd since other than pushing back or turning to face those who shoved him, he hadn't done much to stand up to the bullies.

Bas finally appeared when lunch was almost over, and Adam raised a brow in question to him. What had taken him so long?

"So," Bas said as he sat down. "I've found something to help keep you from being wishy-washy and that will look good on your college applications."

"What?"

He took a piece of paper out of his book bag and set it in front of Adam with a flourish. The paper was actually the school newspaper.

Adam pushed it away. "I've thought about that. But it's always sports. And I don't want to write about sports."

Bas took the paper and folded it to the inside of the last page, which read: *Looking for writers to talk about real-world issues, raise awareness, and connect with readers on a personal level. Like controversy? Want to help others? Section will be part informational, part advice column. Serious thinkers only. Come write for Northern News. See Michelle Young.*

"An advice column?"

"I asked Michelle about it. She said that there will be one whole page each issue dedicated to raising awareness for a cause and another page devoted to answering questions from readers. There is going to be a locked drop box so people can write letters to the column seeking advice. The faculty is actually going to be scanning the stuff put in the box before passing it on. She said she already has a ton, and while a few people have applied for the position, she hasn't found anyone whose writing is up to par." Bas tapped Adam's laptop, which was still open to his ranting of the day. "And I just happened to show her the paper you wrote about how marriage equality was won for interracial couples. I loved how you used a real-life couple to talk about the troubles they fought through until they could finally marry and do something most people take for granted, like joint taxes."

"How'd you get a copy of that?"

"I helped grade it, of course. You don't really think Mrs. Sanders actually reads all three hundred of those papers, right? I mean, they had to be at least five pages long. Yours was almost double that. And since she knows you have no problem with structure, she handed it off to me."

"Thanks for the A."

"You're welcome. It was well deserved. So do you think you can do this newspaper thing?"

Adam flipped through the pages. It was done in more of a magazine style. He read it all the time, usually skipping the sports, which were front-page news, to find out more about the other clubs in the school. The format was a little dull, but maybe he could have some input on that. "How much time is it going to take? Principal O'Brien asked me this morning if I would think about changing to some AP classes next semester. I gotta ask my mom and dad, but I think I will."

"One meeting a week for an hour. The print paper comes out every two weeks, but the online version is updated weekly. So you'll probably spend a lot of time writing outside of school, but I'm pretty sure you do that already." Bas got up from the table, since everyone was leaving. It was almost time for class. "How about I take you to meet her during study hall today? You can hash out any details. And it will give you some time to think."

Adam nodded. Time to think was good. He headed to his next class in an odd fog of indecision. While he liked the idea of writing, putting things out there for other students to raise awareness, he worried about the advice part of it. Who was he to give anyone advice?

CHAPTER 19

RU LANDED in San Diego to a runway full of cameras. He wondered briefly if they'd found out about Adam and that's why the paps were suddenly so pushy, but when he got into the car and flipped open his phone, he realized that had nothing to do with it.

"Sorry, Ru," Katie, his publicist said.

"About what? What happened?" He was on his way to an interview and had planned to get there early enough to get hair and makeup done, call Adam for lunch, and then do the interview.

"Kris has been all over the news. There are rumors that AJ is going to add him to Vocal Growth."

"What? He can't sing and he can't dance. You should have seen him when we went clubbing—he was like an epileptic seal. Plus he's gay, and I got kicked out for being gay." Ru pinched the bridge of his nose, feeling a headache coming on.

"It's just a rumor. But it's running pretty strong. They will probably ask you about it at the interview."

"Whatever. VG is no longer my concern. I'm going to call Tommy. See if he's okay. But I'm on my way to the interview now."

"Keep your cool, no matter what they ask."

"I always do," Ru reminded her and hung up so he could call Tommy. All he got was the man's voice mail. "Dammit, Tommy, where are you?"

Tommy didn't pick up until Ru was finished with hair and makeup and practically headed into the interview room. Unfortunately, he wouldn't have time to call Adam. "Where have you been?" Ru demanded.

"Putting out fires. Sorry." Tommy sounded worn. He had flown down Thursday during the day, but Ru didn't think twenty-four hours was enough time to make a man sound like he was about to fall off a ledge.

"What's all this stuff about Kris going to VG?"

"No idea."

"But you said you're putting out fires."

"I talked to Herb. Wanted to see if there was a chance for me. I know my voice is only okay, but I just didn't want to live in AJ's shadow. Herb said I'm not ready for a solo career."

Ru sucked in a deep breath. "What are you saying?"

"I quit VG."

"But Tommy—"

"It's okay. It will be okay. I was just wondering if maybe I can tour with you for a while. I'm okay with just playing on the board and singing backup. Herb says it will give me more experience, and since I'm working with you on songwriting, maybe you'll help me broaden my skills."

"But if you just do backup for me, that's really no different than doing it for AJ," Ru pointed out.

"Yeah, it is. You're not an asshole. You don't insult me just to get a rise out of me and embarrass me in front of others. So is AJ planning on using Kris in the group? No idea. It would be music suicide, but whatever."

"What happened? I feel like I did this somehow."

"It was my choice. I was at rehearsal yesterday, getting blasted for not learning whatever stupid move. Everyone was laughing at me, and then AJ told me we had an interview next week, but I needed to lose weight to be in the photos. Said I looked too big to be part of VG." Tommy sighed into the phone. "Then I remembered he did that all the time to you. And now you have this horrible body image."

"I do not."

"You do. So I just had it. I told him I was done and that he could find himself another clone to shove up his royal white ass. It felt really good in that moment to tell him off. Now looking back, it's kind of terrifying."

"That you threw it all away in a moment of anger? I'm sure if you asked and begged, they'd let you back in the group," Ru pointed out.

"But I don't want that. I shouldn't have to be begging. We started off as a team. The four of us looked to AJ because he was more social, not because he was better than us. The years have turned him into a monster."

Ru sat in the chair in his dressing room just staring at the far wall, trying to figure it all out. "Where are you? Are you close to downtown?"

"I can be. Whatcha need?"

"How about we do an interview to blow this all up?"

"Are you saying what I think you're saying?"

"Announcing to the world that you've left VG, and are going to tour with me? If that's what you want. If you're sure you're done with VG and AJ. I just don't want you to be doing any of this because of me." Ru wondered if this meant the end for his old group. One member lost, maybe, but two? "The media is going to come down like a storm on both of us. Best to get it over with."

"I know. But I'm okay with it. And yeah, I'm done with VG. It was time to move on anyway. I'm not a kid anymore. I want to have say in the music. I'm tired of dancing those dumb AJ-patented moves. Maybe I'm not a rock star like you, and maybe I'll never do a solo thing. I've been looking at a theater arts program at a few different colleges. Too late for me to get in before next fall, but I figure touring with you will give me more stage time. And that's all I really want, to be on stage."

Ru smiled. The door opened, and someone leaned in to tell him they were ready for him. "Okay, you need to be here in like five minutes if you want to make this official," he told Tommy.

"Let me just find someplace to park and I'll be right up."

They hung up, and Ru got up to make his way to the interview room. He shook hands, smiled, and asked if they wanted an exclusive. Of course they did; everyone wanted to out-scoop everyone else. And so they waited for Tommy, even gave him ten minutes to get through hair and makeup. When they finally sat down to talk, they laid it all on the line.

"So Tommy, you've left Vocal Growth for good?" Their interviewer was a man named Sergio Mateo from one of the largest online music magazines on the West Coast.

"I have. Ryunoski has inspired me to move on."

"What does this mean for your music career?"

"I'll be touring for Ryunoski's debut. Since I'm already recording backup vocals for him, it makes sense. Then I'm going to look into moving to a musical-theater type career."

"And Mr. Nakimura, do you feel you had a hand in this change?"

"Well Tommy's my best friend. I want him to be happy. He's been pretty unhappy with the way Vocal Growth has changed in the past eight months. I want to support him in any way I can. He's family to me," Ru replied. He knew what the next question would be before it was even asked. He'd warned Tommy when they went in that the conversation would turn to his sexuality. Everything was about Ru being gay, though it really had nothing to do with anything at all. The press just loved to talk about it.

"So are you lovers?"

"No," Tommy said.

"No," Ru replied. "He's like my big brother. I am currently in a relationship but not with Tommy. Tommy is still searching for the love of his life and his role in this world. I'm just here to help him anyway I can." He redirected the heat back to himself, figuring Tommy could use a breather, and any good interviewer would want to know more about a confessed new flame.

"So you've got a new lover? Are you willing to talk about him? Is he anyone we know?"

"No, you wouldn't know him. He's not in the spotlight. I'd like to keep the relationship quiet. My time with Kris was heavily tainted by interference from the media. I want to avoid that now if I can. Let me just say that I'm crazy in love with this guy, and I hope we can grow old together. He helped put me back together," Ru answered truthfully. He didn't know if Adam would ever see the interview. Maybe Ru would send it to him.

"Sounds like a very special guy. Was 'Start Something' written for him?" Sergio asked.

"Yes. He is very special. But I think you'll have to realize that I'm only seventeen, and like me, he's very young. I want to protect him as much as I can."

"The media can be harsh. I've heard you've been doing a lot of LGBT benefit shows and even donated a song called 'Bullied,' which is an angst-driven hard rock song unlike anything we've heard from you, to the cause of LGBT youth. Do you feel more connected to these kids because you are gay?"

"I feel more connected to them because I was abandoned. I have never spoken about it to the media before, but when I was eleven, I came out to my father. He couldn't take it. So he left. I don't think people realize how often kids are abandoned by their parents because they are gay, or bi, or trans, or just a little different. And of those kids who are abandoned, a lot of them don't make it. A lot of them commit suicide. That's unacceptable to me—kids killing themselves, kids killing each other, or kids bullying each other to death. That should be unacceptable to everyone." Ru sat back in the chair and thought about some of the things he'd read in Adam's journals. Bullying wasn't just for gay kids, though they did get a lot of it. Everyone was bullied. Even him, a man who had money, power, and fame. It was never good enough. "Everyone needs to know they are loved. That's what it means to be human."

Ru left the interview feeling good. He had a few more to go before he could get back to Adam but knew he could fly through them if he needed too. Tommy, however, looked as worn as he had sounded. "Why don't you go back to my place and sleep for a bit? Let me do some more interviews. I'll call Katie and have her spin it. And you'll probably want to set up a contract with her since you're not with VG anymore. You know she's taken good care of me."

Tommy nodded. "Did you feel like this? Like you're all alone?"

Ru reached out and hugged Tommy. "You're not alone." He watched his friend blink back tears, worried that he just didn't know what to do or what to say. "Let me call Katie to reschedule these two interviews. We'll go to lunch someplace private or just order Thai up to my place. The paps probably have yours covered."

"If you reschedule, it will take you longer to get back to Adam."

"Adam will understand. I'll call him. Now let's go." Ru took Tommy home, called for takeout, and then dialed Katie. She promised to work on rescheduling the interviews. When the food finally came, he and Tommy ate in silence. Ru watched his friend, searching for signs that he needed something else. He remembered the days after he'd been outed and how he wanted nothing more than to hide from the world. The silence of his condo had been a haven for him. Maybe it could help Tommy like that too. "Too bad we don't have Binks here. We could send him to your place to get clothes and stuff."

Tommy laughed lightly. "Yeah, hard to find someone that trustworthy here. Everyone wants to steal my underwear."

"'Cause you have such great taste in underwear or something?" Ru teased.

"So tell me about Wednesday night with Adam," Tommy said, changing the subject. "I left you two alone. You locked the door...."

Ru blushed. He could feel the heat of it warming his face.

"Oh, oh!" Tommy pointed at Ru. "You did something naughty."

"Oh my God, you're like a two-year-old sometimes," Ru complained.

"So talk. No nasty details. But fun was had?"

"Yes, fun was had. It was sweet." He looked away, trying not to get excited just thinking about it. "Amazing. And not just physical."

Tommy set his container aside. "Adam is a great kid. He's been good for you. Making you smile all the time, and showing you how to exercise. I don't think you realize how toned you've become in the past few weeks. I heard the wardrobe lady bitching 'cause your sleeves are getting too tight in the shoulders. Then a second later she was oohing and aahing about how hot you are."

"As if."

"Total truth, man."

Ru sighed. "Yeah, I've gotta find someplace to go when I'm here. I'm so used to running everyday with Adam, it's like my body is a bundle of nervous twitches telling me to get moving. Of course, that could be because I miss him like crazy every second I'm not with him."

"I don't even know where to begin. My building has a private workout room. This one, not so much." Tommy glared at the gray walls. "I never realized how cold it is in here. Not the temperature but the style. It doesn't suit you."

"It works. The furniture is comfy. I can't hear anyone else. It's a good place to be."

Someone knocked on the door. Ru and Tommy exchanged a confused look. "Oh hell no." Tommy said. "If that is a pap, then the next thing you're going to see is me punching some random camera guy. How'd they get past the door guard?" He got up and went to the door. "And why the hell don't you have one of those peephole things in your door?"

"I read something somewhere about a special camera that can be put in those being used to spy on celebrities," Ru told him. "So I made sure I had a door without one."

Tommy opened the door a hair, swore, and then swung it wide. "What the fuck are you doing here?"

Ru expected AJ, but it was Kris who walked in. He gawked at the man he'd spent almost two years with. The guy hadn't changed at all: same top-of-the-line clothes and style, perfect haircut, spiked with frosted tips. Kris crossed the room, heading for Ru. Ru backed away. "Get out of my house."

"So who is it? All I've heard for the last two hours is that Ryunoski Nakimura has moved on, found some sweet nothing to fill his bed. Who?" Kris demanded.

"Since you're not part of my life, what does it matter? Now get out."

"And what was the comment 'he's very young'? Are you trying to say I'm too old for you?"

"You cheated on me. Now get the fuck out of my house." Ru was beginning to lose control of his anger. Last time that happened, he'd punched Nate. He could only imagine the shit storm that would come from him punching Kris.

"Time to go, Turlington." Tommy grabbed his arm. Kris tried to shake him off. "You don't want to start a fight with me. You came here looking for a boost from Ru. You're not getting one. But I'll give you a boost. Right out the fucking door."

"Why do you call him that horrible name? His name is Ryunoski, not Ru. You don't know him at all, Tommy Foster. You're throwing away your career for him. And why? Are the two of you really together? That's what you're hiding? AJ has been telling me that for years." Kris struggled against Tommy, who was pulling him toward the door.

Ru dialed security and demanded they come up to get Kris out immediately, or he was calling the police. When he hung up, he glared at his ex. "So you're here because AJ put you up to it."

Kris shrugged, finally yanking himself free of Tommy's grasp. "All of those pictures, those supposed betrayals, that was all AJ's plan. Hell, he even set us up because he was tired of you getting all the solos and everyone asking for you in interviews. He couldn't find a way to make you quit, so he just made sure the label had a reason to oust you."

"You've got to be kidding," Tommy said. "Don't blame your fame hunt on AJ. He's already got enough sins at his door."

"I've been calling for months, trying to explain all of this. I have proof. Phone calls from him to me. When I replayed the calls for him, he offered me Tommy's spot in Vocal Growth. Said he could make me a star." Kris moved across the room to stand in front of Ru. "But I don't want to be a star. I just want you back. I want to fix what went wrong."

Ru shook his head. "We're over." But the words made him think back to all the stuff in the papers, all the pictures that kept popping up. No one would care if Kris was calling them in. After all, he was just the guy who jilted some boy-band star. But if they came from AJ, well, that gave them weight. Which was why the story never died. The door opened and half a dozen large security guys were there. "Get him out of here, and be sure he doesn't get back into the building."

"Ryunoski, don't do this. I told you the truth. It was all AJ. Even now, he's digging up what he can on this new guy so he can put another nail in your social coffin. He's obsessed with being better than you, and every time you go out in public, people love you more and more."

"Too little, too late," Ru said as the guards grabbed Kris and dragged him out. Ru dialed Katie a second later to fill her in.

"Don't do anything rash," she told him. "Even if it's true, it's in the past."

"What if AJ really goes after Adam?"

"Let me deal with AJ. Do you want me to file a restraining order against Kris?"

"And AJ."

"You're sure about that?"

"Yes."

"Consider it done."

When the quiet was restored, he sank down onto the cushy sweetness of his overstuffed couch. "Wow."

Tommy laughed and plopped himself down next to Ru. "Never realized what a freak that guy was." They sat in silence for a few minutes. "Do you really think it could have been AJ?"

"Makes sense."

"Bastard."

"Agreed."

They bumped fists. Ru sent Adam a text that said he'd call him late. He would need to make sure if reporters found Adam, they wouldn't find him without Ru. No way could Adam handle the daily grind of paps following his every step.

CHAPTER 20

ADAM made it through the rest of the day but only received a single text from Ru. At least he promised to call. When Bas introduced Adam to Michelle, they hit it off and talked for a long while about the importance of the column she wanted to begin in the Northern News. He agreed to do the awareness half, but argued over the advice part of it. In the end he agreed to try it, and if it became too awkward, the section would be cut.

He was on his way out when he ran into Nate. In fact, he'd forgotten all about the homecoming game until that moment. "Hi, Nate," he grumbled as he passed the footballer in the hall.

"So you're going, right?"

Did he really have a choice? "To the game, yes. I will be sitting in the stands with Bas and Michelle." Michelle would be covering the game for the paper. She was crazy enough about sports to make him shake his head and gladly leave that portion to her.

"Michelle? She your beard or something?"

"She's my editor. I joined the paper. You'll check out my first article, won't you? It will be in next Wednesday's issue, about bullying."

"I'm not bullying you."

"Yeah, you are. It's just another form of blackmail. 'Do this my way or I'll hurt you.' But I'm not just talking about me. I'm talking about how you make fun of Bas in the lunchroom and the little person every time she passes your locker. I'm writing about how you ignore your *friends* when they hurt other people. Including last year when you knew Hank was going to beat up Bas in the bathroom. Did you get in a few licks yourself once Bas had been beaten unconscious?"

Nate paled. "I've never hit anyone. Your boyfriend hit me. I'd say he was more a bully than me."

Adam shook his head. "Believe what you will. But yeah, I'll be at the game." With that, he walked away. His dad was waiting in the parking lot to take him to the community center. Just because Ru wasn't there didn't mean he could skip out on running. And knowing he had to show up to watch a team he hated because he was being blackmailed, only made him more jittery.

When seven thirty rolled around and Bas appeared in the driveway to take him to the game, he was feeling pretty calm. Ru hadn't called yet, but Bas had forwarded him a text with a link to an interview Ru had just done. The guy had all-out admitted to being crazy in love with him. Tommy had been there too, talking about how he was leaving Vocal Growth, which made Adam wonder what had happened in the last day since they'd seen each other. He hoped they were both okay.

Michelle insisted they sit near the bottom of the stands, close enough to see the plays and the players who sat on the bench. She was pretty intense to watch the game with, shouting and jumping up all the time. Adam even had Bas switch seats with him. Bas just seemed amused by her jostling. During halftime, Adam headed to the concessions area, not wanting junk food but hungry enough to eat anyway.

"Want something?" he shouted to Bas and Michelle over the music of the marching band.

Michelle shook her head.

Bas handed him a five-dollar bill. "There's a pizza truck by the parking lot; just get a large whatever. We'll share."

"Pizza's good," Adam said and headed off to find the truck. He put in his order and leaned against the truck to wait. Everyone was in the stands cheering on the band.

Nate suddenly appeared at Adam's side. He was sweaty and still in uniform, but smiling wide. "You came."

"Yeah. I told you I would. What are you doing out here? You should be on the field."

"There's another ten minutes of the band playing. I've got time. I wanted to talk to you. See if maybe you want to get together after the game and hang out." Nate glanced around. They were alone, standing off to the side of the pizza truck. Adam really hoped his order would be up soon so he could grab the food and head back to his seat.

"I don't think that's a good idea. Don't you have to go to the dance with your girlfriend?"

"She won't mind if I'm a little late."

"Late? I thought you said you wanted to hang. Never mind. I keep forgetting I'm talking to you, and you never make any sense. You should probably get back to your team. The coach may have some last-minute advice for you," Adam said as Nate pressed closer.

Nate leaned forward, getting into Adam's space and putting Adam's back to the wall. "Did you see me score that last touchdown? We're going to win tonight. Thanks for coming."

"You're welcome. But you know this makes us even, right? No more talk about Ru."

"That guy is not good enough for you."

"What the hell, Nate? I don't get you at all." Adam backed away, coming around the front of the truck, not liking how Nate stalked him. "I think you need to go."

Suddenly Nate grabbed him, yanked him forward, and mashed his lips to Adam. Ten seconds of stunned submission passed before Adam shoved Nate away. His heart hammered in his chest, and he no longer cared about pizza or the rest of the night. He needed to go home, to talk to Ru, to feel secure again. But Nate wasn't about to free him. He shoved Adam against the wall of the truck, holding him there. Nate ground Adam's right wrist into the metal wall, hard enough to hurt. "You're such a damn cock tease. I've waited almost two months for you. Played your little games. Time to let go of the innocent act. Let me show you a good time. You don't need that singer."

"You're doing all this because you want me?" Adam couldn't believe what he was hearing, couldn't believe that Nate had just kissed him. "Have you been stalking me from the beginning for this? All the demands to run with you, and you couldn't just have said, 'Hey, Adam, I'm gay too, wanna go out?'"

Nate's grip on Adam's wrist tightened to keep him from running. "I'm not gay. Not like you or Bas or that guy you're with. Besides, my life would be over. I'd never get into the U on a football scholarship. And I'm not stopping there. I will be recruited to the NFL. Just wait. A year, maybe two, but I'll have a couple-million dollar salary. We can be together in private. Run after school when the team isn't practicing. Have some private time in the locker room. It's okay."

"You've got to be kidding me. Get off me." Adam struggled to pull out of Nate's grasp, only gaining an inch or two. But the footballer squeezed tighter, fighting with him until he slammed Adam's arm back against the side of the truck. Adam felt something pop and a sharp pain shoot up his wrist. "Let go!"

"We were a great team before he came. But then you stopped running with me. You didn't want me anymore. Was it the money? I've got money. I can buy you nice things." He dragged Adam away from the light and toward the shadowed edge cast by the truck.

Adam tugged on his wrist, trying to free himself, fear and desperation starting to rise fast enough to make him nauseous. "We're not doing this. We're not even friends, Nate. I wouldn't date you if you paid me."

Nate shoved him against the truck again, hard enough to make a loud noise that disturbed the guys inside. "Hey!" they shouted. But Nate held him there a minute longer before pulling away.

Adam finally yanked himself free when Nate's grip loosened. His wrist was throbbing. "No more, Nate. In school, if you see me, you walk the other way. Don't talk to me. Don't text me. Just pretend I don't exist." He backed away slowly, afraid the footballer would attack him again.

"You're not listening to me," Nate said.

"Adam?" Bas called. "Everything okay?" He appeared in front of Adam, putting himself between them, like he knew something had gone down. He glanced up at the guy in the pizza truck, who held a box out. Apparently their food was ready, but Adam had lost his appetite.

"I need to go home," Adam whispered, clinging to Bas—not realizing before that moment that Bas was taller than him—and watching Nate with wide eyes. Hank and Jonah arrived a minute later, only to immediately begin shouting things at them. "Please, please, Bas. Just take me home."

"Okay. We're going." Bas grabbed the pizza and headed toward the parking lot, his arm protectively around Adam's shoulders. Michelle caught up with them as they reached the car. "You can stay if you want, but I need to take Adam home. I'll come back later to pick you up."

"It's okay, Bas. I'll find a ride. Everything okay?" They both stared at Adam, but no one spoke until Michelle nodded. "Have a good night, Adam. Let me know if you need something."

He needed Ru. Could anyone get the man for him? He was half a country away, and Adam needed him. By the time they were on the road to Adam's home, he'd begun to shake. The memory of being shoved against the truck, the pain in his arm, and being held down really scared him. "Did you know?" Adam finally asked Bas.

"That Nate is gay and thinks he's not? Yeah. That he wants you? Yeah. I warned you a couple times, if you remember. I saw the way he looked at you."

"But I didn't do anything. I didn't like lead him on or anything. I told him we're not even friends." Adam wondered how all this could happen. And yet it all made so much sense. Why Nate's jockstrap friends didn't want Adam around. Why they always gave him a hard time. They all knew. "He wanted me to be some kind of secret lover or something. How could I be so blind?"

"You're not blind. Nate's not a good guy. Don't let what he does mess with your head."

"Was he there? That night when they beat you in the bathroom?"

Bas was silent for a minute. "We had a thing going on. It was pretty one-sided. I would meet him there, blow him. He never returned the favor. I thought, hey, the most popular guy in school is attracted to me. But he wasn't; he used me. That night he told me to meet him, only he wasn't there—Hank was."

"That's awful." Adam's head hurt. He just wanted to crawl under the covers and forget this horrible night. "Is that what he wanted me to be? Just some body to use? He said he'd never get a scholarship if they thought he was gay, that we could be together in private. How did I not see this?"

"I'm sorry, Adam. I never thought he'd hurt you physically. After that night, he just ignored me. It was like I only existed after that as someone he could torment when he was around his friends." Bas pulled the car into Adam's driveway. "Do you want me to come in with you?"

"No." Adam left the pizza with Bas. "I'll see you next week. I just want to go in and talk to my parents and maybe call Ru."

"Okay. Call or text if you need me. I'm sorry again. I probably should have been more straightforward with you about what happened between Nate and me. But it's kind of embarrassing. He left me feeling used, even more than being found half-naked on the bathroom floor did." Bas stared out the opposite window. Adam just nodded, got out, and waved him off.

By the time Adam got inside, his wrist was really aching. The skin around it was a burst of angry red, purple, and blue. Not good. "Mom, Dad?" he called, hoping they were still up. Did he sound as freaked out as he felt?

His dad appeared in the living room first. "What happened?" He crossed the room in two long strides. "You're shaking. What happened?"

Adam couldn't hold back anymore. He let his dad's arms surround him and just cried. He didn't care he was sixteen and it wasn't cool to be taken care of by his mom and dad. He just wanted to feel safe again.

He ended up in the emergency room with a fractured bone in his wrist. Most of the night became a blissful blur when they gave him drugs to numb him before they set the bone in place. Adam's dad had asked a hundred questions, most of which Adam answered but could barely remember by the time they were headed home. He did remember texting Ru, begging his boyfriend to come back, though he couldn't recall what he said exactly.

There were several pings to his phone, but the fog of drugs and pain kept him from reaching for it. By the time his parents tucked him into bed and had given him a second dose of medication it was after 4:00 a.m., and Adam was out as soon as his head hit the pillow.

His phone ringing was the first thing to wake him that Saturday morning. He glared at the clock, realizing it was after ten. He never slept that late, but reached for the phone anyway, only to be reminded that his right wrist was in a thick cast. He sighed, grabbed the phone with his left instead, and hit Answer. It was Bas.

"Did you see the links I sent you? I don't know how to stop it. I don't know who posted it."

"Huh? Slow down. I think my head is still fuzzy from the drugs," Adam grumbled.

"Drugs? You're doing drugs?"

"Just painkillers the doctor gave me. Nate broke my wrist." He floundered around for a minute until he could balance the phone between his ear and shoulder and pull himself into a sitting position with his left arm. He'd have to work on that one more. It shouldn't have felt so weak compared to what he normally did with his right, but he was right-handed, so maybe he was just used to holding or lifting things longer.

"What? Why didn't you tell me? I would have taken you to the hospital."

"My parents took me. So it's fine. Now what are you talking about, links and stopping something? What was posted?"

"Someone got a picture of you and Nate kissing. It's all over Facebook. Well, it's mostly you. Can't really make out Nate's face in the picture, though you can kinda see the Northern High football uniform he's wearing."

The words took a minute to sink in before Adam could understand what he was saying. "Wait. So you're telling me someone got a picture of Nate assaulting me but couldn't actually come help? I seriously doubt I look all that willing. He kept shoving me around."

"It's a picture, Adam. Not a video. Means it is one second of your life that the whole world is analyzing. Everyone's going on and on about who else is in the photo with you."

The thought suddenly struck him: what if Ru saw it? What if Ru thought it was just like his last boyfriend all over again? "I have to talk to Ru. He'll think I'm like Kris. That I'm cheating on him." His heart pounded, and it was really hard to breathe. He jumped out of bed and began struggling into clothes. "Maybe I can convince my parents to let me fly to San Diego. I can talk to Ru before he sees it, tell him it wasn't something I wanted."

"Sweetie, you have a broken wrist to prove you didn't want it. What are you going to do about Nate?"

"What can I do? Avoid him, probably."

"Did you tell your parents?"

Had he? He couldn't remember much about last night once the fog of drugs had taken over. The setting of the bone of his wrist was just a vague memory, like something he'd seen on a TV show once, instead of something that had really happened to him. "I need to go. I gotta talk to Ru."

"Okay, call me."

Adam headed into the bathroom, brushed his teeth, and ran a comb through his tangled hair. He heart hadn't stopped racing by the time he made his way downstairs. He heard his parents talking in the kitchen, the sound of dishes, and pots being stirred. They were making breakfast and his world was falling apart?

But when he stepped into the kitchen, it wasn't just his parents. Ru sat at the counter with Tommy and a blonde woman who Adam had never met. Tears filled Adam's eyes as he looked at Ru. Was he here to end it? Would the past two months just be over like they were some unattainable dream?

"Adam, sit down. You look like you're about to fall over. Let your mom get you some breakfast. Do you need another pain pill?" his dad called to him.

Ru got up from the chair and crossed the room to wrap his arms around Adam. For the second time in less than twenty-four hours, Adam was reduced to a sobbing mess. "I didn't kiss him," he kept saying, trying to assure Ru that he wouldn't cheat.

Several minutes passed before Adam pulled through enough of his panic to finally hear Ru talking to him. "Breathe, baby. Just like you're running. In and out, deep breaths. I know you wouldn't cheat.

It's okay. We're fixing this. Just calm down for me, okay? I'm here. You wanted me to be here, and I'm here. Shh."

"You know I didn't kiss him?" Adam pulled away, wiping his eyes and runny nose on his shirtsleeve. He probably looked awful, and yet Ru was there, holding him, running his hands soothingly down his arms and back.

"Come sit down and we'll talk about all this, okay? You need some food in you, and I'm pretty sure you need one of those pain pills your dad was talking about. How's your wrist? Does it hurt?" Ru coaxed Adam to sit at the counter with the rest of them. Adam's mom handed him a damp towel, which Ru used to wipe Adam's face clean. "Better?"

Adam nodded and gulped back a dozen words he wanted to say but knew would set him off again.

"We'll talk after breakfast if you feel up to it. But food first." Ru shoved a plate of eggs and bacon toward Adam. "You eat, okay?"

"Okay."

"I got your text. You didn't answer when I called, and your text was weird. I called your dad, who told me what happened. So I got on a plane. Arrived a couple hours ago. Your folks said you were still sleeping, so we stopped at Tommy's and had a short nap." He glanced at Tommy and the blonde woman with them. "Tommy wanted to come too, needs some time away, and he was worried when I told him what happened. And Katie," he said, motioning to the blonde, "is here to put out fires. Our former bandmate AJ is on a smear crusade against me. And it looks like he's already got his hands on that photo and is selling it to magazines saying you're cheating on me."

"But I'm not!" Adam insisted. "I wouldn't ever!"

Ru put his finger to Adam's lips. "Shh, baby. I know. That's why Katie is here. She's been talking to your parents about different options. Ways to approach this. Either way, you're going to be outed as my boyfriend. That is, if you still want to be my boyfriend."

Adam gripped Ru's hand with his good left one. "Don't be stupid."

"That's what I keep telling him," Tommy said.

Adam's dad reached out to squeeze Adam's arm. "You let us take care of this. Eat, go spend time with Ru. Once you're done, we'll have a plan. Just this once, let us be the grown-ups, okay?"

"Okay." He glared at his cast, hating that it made it impossible to hold Ru's hand. The truth was he didn't want to eat. He didn't want to run. He just wanted to be wrapped up in Ru's arms and sleep for the next couple of years. But Ru seemed to have other plans for him.

CHAPTER 21

EARLIER that day, Ru was eating dinner when the text arrived from Adam. *Help! Need u. Please come. Please!*

"What is it?" Tommy asked. The two had found a nearby gym to try, one that had private areas to cater to clients who wanted solitude. And they had a full indoor track that Ru knew Adam would have loved. Tommy even remarked that Ru "ran his ass off." The intense workout made them hungry, so they returned to Ru's place and ordered food.

"A text from Adam, but it's weird. I need to call him." He dialed the familiar number, but it just rang and rang. He sent a text and tried to call again. "He's not answering."

"It's what, after ten? Not that late for a Friday night. Maybe he's out with friends?"

Ru shook his head. Adam was a homebody. If he wasn't out running, he was home in the quiet comfort his parents provided. "I wonder if I saved his dad's number." He scrolled through his Saved list and found it, dialed, but again got voice mail. This time he left a message. "Hey, Mr. Corbin, it's Ru. I got a weird text from Adam, and I'm worried. Is he home with you? Please call me. Thanks."

He hung up, glared at the phone, then dialed Adam again. Still no answer. "What if something happened to him?"

"Ru, you can't freak out just 'cause he's out of touch for a few minutes. Give it an hour and then try again." Tommy began cleaning up the dishes and putting things away.

"His text said 'help,' Tommy. He needs me. He wants me to come to him. I need to go pack." Ru headed to his bedroom and began throwing things in a bag.

"A half an hour. Just give him a little time. What if you show up, and he's embarrassed 'cause he meant something completely different? What if he's just freaking out because he hasn't talked to you all day?"

"I should have insisted he come with me. Then he'd be here with me now."

"And would have had to run into Kris. In case you forgot, the kid nearly had a heart attack just from seeing the old picture of you and Turlington. He's got it so bad for you, he probably would have ripped Kris apart right there in your living room."

Ru dialed Adam again. Still no answer. "What if AJ got to him?"

"And did what? Told the media, 'Hey, there's this sweet little high schooler that happens to have captured the heart of Ryunoski Nakimura, my arch nemesis. Go look at him'? The paps would give it like ten seconds when they saw you weren't there with him." Tommy grabbed Ru's hands. "Twenty minutes. I'll even set the timer on the microwave. If he's still not picking up, then we call Katie and head back to Minnesota. You do realize that it's a four-hour flight, so even if we get on a plane, you won't be there for a while."

"But I'll be on the way." Ru stared at the text. Help? Was he hurt? Was he in danger? Tommy led Ru to the couch, and they sat down together waiting for either the phone to ring or the timer to beep. It was the longest twenty minutes of Ru's life. He nearly jumped a half foot off the couch when the beep sounded, even though he'd been waiting for it. He dialed Adam again, no answer, then Katie, who picked up immediately. She listened to his worried rant and how he had to go. She didn't even try to talk him out of it, just told him she would meet him at the airport.

Tommy had a bag packed, Ru's in hand, and grabbed the guitar before the conversation was even over. "I swear if he's just having a 'miss Ru' moment I'm going to smack him," Tommy grumbled.

The ride to the airport took almost an hour. Ru just wanted to be there. He had little patience for the scanning and probing done at the airport. Even getting an escort didn't help ease his growing aggression.

It was just taking too long. Katie waited for them at the gate, having chartered a private plane that belonged to Ru's label. Just as they got settled into their seats, Ru's phone rang.

"Is it Adam?" Tommy asked.

Ru glanced at the display, and his heart lurched in fear. "Mr. Corbin? Is Adam okay?"

"There was an incident at school, but Adam is going to be fine. He was a little loopy when he sent you that text earlier. We're going to leave the hospital in a little while, just as soon as they are sure he's reacting okay to the pain medication."

"Hospital? Pain medication? What happened?"

The captain announced they would be taking off.

"Are you on a plane?" Mr. Corbin asked.

"I got a text from my boyfriend asking for help, telling me that he needed me. Yes, I'm on a plane. We'll be arriving sometime after three your time." He probably shouldn't have snapped at Adam's dad, but he just needed to be there. Especially since his worst fear had come true, and Adam was hurt.

"Okay. We'll talk when you're on the ground. The doctor is calling me back in the room now, and you should turn off your phone for the flight."

"But I need to hear from Adam."

"When you get here. No need to let you stew on it all until then. Just know he's going to be fine." Mr. Corbin hung up. Ru sighed and turned the phone off.

"What happened? He's in the hospital?"

"I don't know what happened. He just said that Adam was okay, but that they were in the hospital and checking to make sure his pain medicine was all right." He ground his teeth together. Someone had hurt Adam, and he had a sneaking suspicion who. And while there was nothing he could do until he got there, he wasn't going to let anyone get away with it.

He dozed on the plane, jerking awake a few times from nightmares. The last time he was so shaken he had to get up and move a little. The small plane didn't have much space to roam, but he walked back and forth for several minutes, trying to calm his pounding heart.

Tommy slept curled up in his chair, a blanket pulled up around him in a way that meant someone else must have put it there. But Katie was awake. She glared at her phone like it was going to bite her. Ru dropped into the seat beside her. "What?"

"AJ found Adam."

"What? How do you know?" Ru tried to look at the screen of her phone to read what she was seeing.

"I have a friend at one of the celebrity rags. She forwarded me this." Katie turned the phone his way. It was a picture of Adam kissing someone else. Not just someone else, *Nate.*

"What the hell?"

"Don't get all upset over this, Ru."

"What do you mean, don't get upset?" How could he have let himself trust Adam? Didn't he remember how much it hurt the last time? *Oh God.*

"Stop rolling this over in your head, Ru. Adam's not cheating on you. Look at his posture in this picture. He's on the defense. And the bigger guy has got a pretty solid grip on him." Katie thrust the picture closer.

Ru studied it for the things he normally saw from Adam, but everything about the young man said he was being forced. Forced. "You don't think that's what happened, do you? That he's in the hospital because Nate forced him to…." Ru couldn't even think the word. "Oh my God. I knew that guy was a freak, but I never thought he'd actually do something like that." Once again Ru was back to pacing the plane. He tugged mercilessly on his hair, wanting to rip it out because he was there, flying over the middle of nowhere, and not close enough to help Adam. "I shouldn't have left him."

"This is not your fault. And truly, if it were that serious, wouldn't his father have been more worried?" Katie as always was the rational voice. She tugged him back down into the chair beside her and ran her fingers through his hair to straighten the mess. "Adam's dad said he'd be okay, right?"

"Yes."

"He didn't say anything about there being something awful they needed to tell you when you got there? Or suggesting that Adam might need counseling?"

"No. He just said he didn't want me to stew on it."

"So don't. As soon as we land, we'll call and find out where they are. Now sit down and get some sleep."

"I can't. Every time I close my eyes, I dream something horrible has happened to him."

Katie grabbed his backpack off the floor and dug through it like the pro she was. A few seconds later she handed him his songbook. "So write it out. But we have another hour in the air."

The jumble that Ru put to page might never become a song, a lot like his sailor rant. But Herb had told him to keep writing even if it was about spiders. So Ru just let it all out. He filled pages with aggressive angry words, fear of not being there, and some unknown curse that seemed to follow him. He was halfway through composing the score when the plane finally set down. The second they were taxiing to the gate, Katie had Adam's dad on the phone.

"I understand. Of course. Call us as soon as he wakes up. Thank you."

"What?" Ru demanded when she hung up.

Tommy stretched and looked at them sleepily. "We there?"

"We're going to Tommy's place."

"But I have to see Adam!" Ru was about to go nuts.

"Adam is asleep. His dad just put him to bed. He's going to call as soon as he wakes up. Now let's go get some sleep ourselves. We'll see them in the morning." Katie glanced at her watch. "Well, later in the morning."

"What happened?" Ru demanded.

"Not much," Katie said. "Not what you're thinking. It didn't go very far, though it did scare Adam pretty bad. He was at the Homecoming game with some friends. Someone named Bas?" Ru nodded. "Apparently Nate cornered Adam when he went to get food. Got a little pushy. Bas went looking for Adam, so they got interrupted.

It wasn't anything more than the kiss and, well, Nate broke Adam's wrist."

"What?" Ru cried.

"What the fuck!" Tommy said.

"But Adam's okay. Bas got him home, and Adam's parents took him to the hospital. He's pretty drugged up on painkillers." Katie looked at Ru. "You need to calm down. I don't think you know just how difficult this is gonna be for Adam. He needs you to hold it together. When he was panicking, he was begging for you to be there."

"And I wasn't. I was in San Diego when I should have been with him."

"Ru, that's not what I meant. What I mean is that he needs you now. He'll need you to be normal, to do day-to-day things with him. Go to get pizza. Watch a movie. Do normal things so he knows his whole world hasn't been messed up by this guy." Katie grabbed Ru's guitar. "Play for him. Sing him 'Start Something' again. His head is going to be so messed up from this."

"What about Nate? We can't let him get away with hurting Adam. And AJ is just going to make it worse by putting it in the papers."

"Not true. I have a dozen people out working on killing the story by telling the truth—that it was a school bully and an assault. The more AJ pushes this, the worse it looks for him."

"Oh my God." Ru nearly swallowed his tongue. "I gotta see Adam."

Tommy put his hand on Ru's shoulder. "We'll stop by Adam's house. Just look in on him, then head back to my place for some sleep, okay?" He gave Katie a tight smile. "You know he won't rest until he sees Adam."

"Fine. But one of you is sleeping on the couch since you're keeping me up so late." Katie pulled Ru into a hug as they made their way out of the airport. "Let's go check on your boy."

Ru spent almost ten minutes just watching Adam sleep before finally agreeing to leave. He wanted to just take the bed in the spare room, or better yet, wrap himself around Adam, but Mr. Corbin suggested that Adam might be too jumpy for that right now. When they got back to Tommy's loft, it was after 5:00 a.m., and Ru barely remembered falling asleep before Katie was shaking him awake.

"Is he up yet?" Ru asked. It was almost nine.

"No. But I'm going to head over and talk some things over with the Corbins. This is going to have media whether we want it to or not." Katie had a stack of papers in hand. Tommy looked more awake than Ru felt, but he'd also slept on the plane and in the car.

"So what is the plan?" Tommy wanted to know as they got in the limo, with Binks at the wheel, and headed back to Adam's house.

"It sounds like the Corbins are going to press charges. They've already been up and talking to the principal of the school and some of the school board members. Northern has a no-bullying policy, and Nate's actions were seen not only by a couple of kids at school, but by the guys working in a food truck that had been hired for Homecoming." Katie pulled out her iPhone and answered a few calls on the way. "I believe they've threatened to pull Adam out of school unless Nate is expelled."

"But Nate's the quarterback. And I checked the Northern High website last night. Looks like they won," Tommy pointed out.

"It will be for the school to decide. Adam's a very good student, and he's well-liked by most of the student body and the faculty. He may not be the most popular kid in school, but everyone knows who he is." Katie reached out to brush Ru's hair back. "And all that is him, and nothing to do with you. So making your relationship public isn't going do anything bad to him."

"You're sure? The paps aren't going to come pounding on his door?" Ru wondered if that was just something they did to Kris.

"No guarantees on that. But because of the nature of the assault, and the fact that both Adam and Nate are minors, most of the papers are killing the story that AJ fed them. I think if the two of you put a positive face to your relationship, the rest of this stuff is going to die pretty fast."

"How are we going to do that?"

Katie grinned. "First, the two of you are going to go on a very public double date at Dimitri's with a LGBT reporter who's been dying for an exclusive. I already talked to Ryan Hart, and he's agreed to bring his partner of four years to dinner for an interview. The meeting should be pretty unintrusive, and I trust Ryan to keep it positive. He's been covering all of your LGBT youth appearances, buying tickets for the different areas you're in, and handing them out to kids in need. I just need to talk to the Corbins, get their okay. Just because you're legally able to make your own decisions doesn't mean Adam is."

Ru nodded. "Adam's folks are great. They take really good care of him."

Tommy messed up Ru's hair. "And you too. I can't wait to eat some of that home cooking you've been telling me about. And don't you dare say I can't come to dinner too."

As soon as Adam was awake and calmed down, Ru was given leave to whisk him away for a few hours. Only Ru took him to Tommy's loft. "Follow me," he said, leading Adam through the condo to Tommy's master bath. "How are you feeling?"

"Tired," Adam grumbled. "Pain medicine is good but makes me sleepy."

"Okay, so a little soaking, then we'll take a nap, 'kay?"

"Soak? I can't get my cast wet." He waved around the bright green wrapped arm. "Wonder why my dad picked green."

"Probably 'cause the other choice was pink." Ru opened the bag of stuff he'd grabbed from the Corbin's house and proceeded to cover Adam's cast in plastic and duct tape. "You wear boxers today?"

Adam blushed. "Boxer briefs."

"'Kay. Off with the rest, then, and into the Jacuzzi." On his way to turn the small heated pool on, he stripped off his shirt and stepped out of his jeans, leaving just his boxers. The small jets erupted in a mass of heated bubbles when he turned the dial to give them a half an hour. "Tommy rarely uses the tub, and I was thinking you could use some relaxing."

Adam undressed slowly and made his way to the Jacuzzi. "It's big."

"Seats twelve." Ru stepped in, sighing at the sweetness of the heat. He held his hand to Adam. "Come on, just warm water and snuggles, I promise." He guided Adam to a seat and sat on his left side just so he could hold his hand. "See? Good, right?"

"Warm." Adam leaned against Ru. "Thank you for coming back. I'm sorry I interrupted your work."

Ru transferred Adam's hand to his left and wrapped his right arm around his boyfriend. "It's just work. It will still be there. I talked to Katie about doing more phone or Skype interviews instead of flying everywhere. And there are plenty of recording studios within walking distance from here. So much is digital now that I can send a lot of it back to Herb without leaving."

"Hmm," Adam mumbled sleepily.

Ru took the time to look him over, noting each bruise or scrape and hoping that whatever they did to Nate, it was bad. He wondered about the double date that would out them as a couple to the world and worried people would bother Adam because of him. "You know I love you, right, Adam?"

"Love you too." Adam smiled at him. They sat together in silence until the jets shut off. Then Ru shuffled Adam out of the hot tub and back to Ru's room, carrying their clothes. Adam didn't even protest about Ru helping him change into dry boxers, then the two curled up in Ru's big bed and went to sleep. They would have time later to worry about what was going to happen with the rest of the world.

CHAPTER 22

THE weekend with Ru flew by. By the time Monday morning was rolling around, the incident from Friday night was a minor memory. Adam spent a lot of time with Ru, eating with him, Tommy, and his parents, exploring the Twin Cities, and snuggling with Ru in front of a couple of good action movies. Adam finished two new articles for the Northern News, got them back from Michelle with edits, and returned them for publication soon after. But for all the excitement and peace he had over the weekend, he dreaded returning to school. Would Nate be there? What about Jonah and Hank?

Adam's parents had taken over most of the discussion about what would happen with Nate, only consulting him for small things, like Bas' phone number, and to retrieve the stack of notes Adam had kept from those slipped in his locker. He had no idea what to expect come Monday morning, but Ru took him to school. Adam felt like a baby for wanting to cling, but the sight of the campus and the front edge of where the parking lot joined up to the football field made his heart pound in remembered fear.

"You call me if you need anything. I'm going to be at the library." Ru pointed to the college campus across the way, the place they first met. "I'll even meet you for lunch."

"Okay. I'm sorry to be such a baby."

Ru laughed, but it was a bitter sound. "Nothing to be sorry about. I should have been here. I should have warned you. This should be just like any other day for you. It's my fault it's not. If I had been here, you wouldn't have gone to the game. You'd have been home snuggling with me."

"It wasn't your fault," Adam insisted. He'd watched Ru struggle with it all weekend. "Not either of our faults. Bad things just sometimes happen. We just have to learn how to get past this bump and on to the next." He ran his hand down Ru's cheek, loving the feeling of having him so close. "Kiss me so I can get going."

"'Kay," Ru consented, and Adam leaned into the kiss, wishing the moment could last forever. "See you at lunch. Love you."

Adam smiled as he got out of the car. The cold finally hit him now that he was without Ru's warmth. "Love you too." He watched the car move toward the college campus and made his way inside. He'd purposely arrived early so he wouldn't run into as many people in the halls. Bas, however, was waiting for him just inside the entry.

"You two are so cute!" Bas nearly squealed. "I can't believe you're dating *the* Ryunoski Nakimura. Have you heard him sing? Sets my loins atingling every time."

"Did you just tell me what I think you just told me?" Adam asked.

Bas blushed. "Sorta just popped out. I've been reading a lot of romance novels. Sorry."

"Forgiven. So what are you doing here so early?"

"Getting ready for the assembly."

"Do I need to ask?" Adam had a feeling it had something to do with him. "Is it about me?"

"It's actually about bullying. Your article about bullying is already up on the Northern site. I know 'cause I posted it." Bas grinned. "Michelle hired me as the new web guy since it was taking her forever to do. So I redesigned the site and have it ready for easy updates. She said you have another article about teen responsibility. I can't wait to read it."

"I finished the edits late last night and e-mailed it to her. She probably hasn't gotten to it yet. So tell me more about this assembly. They aren't going to call me up, are they?" Adam shivered at the thought. He was working on a piece that featured him and Ru coming out together to the school, showing themselves as just a normal couple, despite Ru's fame. Michelle had already promised it would be front page news the week their interview with Ryan Hart went public.

"Principal O'Brien asked me to talk about bullying and the national suicide rate. Spent all weekend on it. Made it heartbreaking and shocking, as it should be. Everyone is going to be broken up by grade. Yours is right after Advisory. Seniors are last because half the upperclassmen are in private meetings with faculty." Bas walked with him to their lockers. "I want to ask, and not sound like a jerk for doing so, but are you doing okay?"

Adam nodded. "Ru helped a lot. Kept me up and moving so I couldn't spend a lot of time agonizing over it. We did so much this weekend. Even went shopping at MoA." The Mall of America was a mecca for those who loved shopping, which Adam did not. Ru's disguise worked pretty well, and all he wore was a baseball cap. The things he had bought for Adam were clothes for the photo shoot and interview they had coming up. The bright colors and snug-fitting outfits weren't things Adam normally wore, but he had to admit he looked good in them. And after staring at himself in the mirror, he realized he felt good about the way he looked. Like that confident kid in the mirror was who he really was.

"Couture is good," Bas said.

Adam opened his locker and pulled out just a folder and some paper, since he'd be going to an assembly right away. Maybe he could do some writing in Advisory. "I'm going to be in some national magazine. So I sorta needed something that didn't make me look like some high school dork."

"Magazine? Hmm. Sweetie, I hope you know that the boy-next-door thing you've got going on is hotter than anything in a magazine." Bas walked with him. "Don't let anything change that."

"Are you saying you have a thing for me?" Adam asked. He'd missed a lot recently. Was that something else he should have been paying attention to? Was he breaking Bas's heart?

"Oh no, honey. Sweet as you are, pretty as you are, my buttons are not pushed. But a guy can dream, right? Everyone dreams of finding that special someone. You're just not that someone for me." He sighed dramatically. "Now if you find that fine Tommy Foster has been hiding some queer secrets in his closet, you point him in my direction."

Adam laughed and shook his head. "You are so over-the-top. But thanks. I appreciate it."

"Anytime. See you later, okay?"

"Meet me outside for lunch, and you can sit with me and Ru."

"So there, sweetie!"

Adam waved good-bye and made his way into the empty classroom. He opened his folder and began to write about Bas, his odd humor, and how uplifting it could be. His pen moved with little coaxing, and soon he had nearly two pages, and the classroom was starting to fill up. Someone sat down next to him, and Adam's spine stiffened. He glanced over, trying to remember the guy's name.

"Hey," he said.

"Hey," Adam replied with the expected straight-boy nod.

"I'm Dustin."

Adam finally looked up, studying the boy, who didn't appear threatening or otherwise misleading. He just sort of looked a little shy and nerdy, with oversized glasses, messy short brown hair, and a short-sleeve button-up shirt. "Adam."

"I know. You're sort of a legend. Standing up to Nate. And that article about bullying was great. Grown-ups don't get it, but you nailed it. It's not that we don't want to tell. It's just that we can't, 'cause we know it will get worse. I never thought about the fact that just facing them, looking them in the eye, might stop it. It's brilliant."

"Wow. Well, thanks. I guess."

More people piled into the class. A lot of them called out "Hello" to Adam, who just threw them a tight smile and a wave. Were they all for real? A few days ago they'd been staring at him like he was the class freak; now they all wanted to be friends? He sighed and went back to writing.

"So I was wondering…," Dustin leaned over and whispered, making Adam tense. "Can you introduce me to your friend Sebastian?"

"Why?" Adam demanded. "He's had enough trouble at this school."

Dustin glanced around the room and then back, his face turning a little red. "I kind of like him. You know, like, *like* like him. I'm even in two of the same classes as him, but he never glances my way."

Adam blinked at Dustin for a minute, trying to make sense of the words coming his way. "Oh. Um. Maybe. I will talk to him." That was Bas' decision to make, though Adam had no problem pointing the guy out.

The loudspeaker clicked, letting them know there was going to be an announcement. A second later Principal O'Brien's voice came over the loudspeaker. "Will all of the junior class proceed to the auditorium, please, for an assembly."

Everyone in Advisory glanced around, searching each other's faces for a reason they were first. Probably because Adam was a junior and this had all started with him. He hoped it ended with him too. He got up from his chair and headed for the auditorium, not caring that everyone else was taking their time.

He made his way to the front row, sat down, and pulled out his pen and paper. Michelle sat down beside him a minute later, then Dustin from Advisory. Even knowing what it was about didn't prepare Adam for the visuals Bas had created. When the lights were lowered, a map of the USA appeared, then a picture of a kid, girl or guy. The screen flashed through them really fast, attaching faces to states and shrinking them down to fit. The progression started slow and began to build faster and faster, filling up states with dots of faces until the map was covered, state lines vanishing.

Bas stepped up as the map finally stopped. "Every year almost five thousand students commit suicide." He pointed to the map. "Those are the kids who died last year. For every death, there are a hundred other attempts. Fourteen percent of you have considered it. And do any of you know why?"

The map changed to a picture of a big guy pushing a smaller guy into a wall of lockers.

"Seventy-seven percent of high school students claim to be bullied. One hundred sixty thousand kids stay home from school every day because they fear being bullied. Kids who are bullied are more likely to commit suicide than one who isn't. And suicide is the third leading killer of those under eighteen." Bas took a deep breath as the picture changed again, this time to images of him right after the beating he took last year.

"Last year I was cornered in the school bathroom and beaten by three jocks who didn't like the fact that I am gay. I lost so much blood that I almost died. If I hadn't been found by a friend who went and got help, I would have died. Others had come and gone, ignoring my cries for help and the blood on the floor." He paused and looked up toward the light like he was trying to keep himself together. "After I got out of the hospital, all I could think about was having to return here, to the place where not only was I bullied almost to death, but where people ignored my pain. I tried twice to kill myself. First by swallowing a bottle of pills, but thankfully my grandmother caught me and rushed me to have my stomach pumped, which is awful if you've never had it done. The second was the night before I was to return to school."

He picked up the microphone and walked toward the front edge of the stage. "I had locked myself in the bathroom with nothing but my phone and a knife. I was sitting there crying, totally terrified of the prospect of stepping through those doors and passing those jocks every day. Terrified, humiliated, and tired. So tired. We all spend our young lives trying to fit in, forcing ourselves to be like everyone we hate just so we don't end up being the guy who gets thrown into the dumpster, or shoved into the lockers, or have things thrown at them at lunch. I was just done."

Bas glanced at Adam and smiled. "Now, he probably doesn't remember this. But this guy called me that night, just as I was putting the knife to my wrist. I remember glancing at my phone and thinking 'Who the hell would call me?' No one likes me, no one cares what happens to me, but there was this guy calling me. I answered, ready to hear some horrible slur against my sexuality or something. But you know what he said? He asked if I was feeling well enough to go get ice cream with him." He shook his head as if the memory itself was unbelievable. But Adam remembered that night pretty vividly. When Bas had arrived to pick him up, he had still looked badly bruised and vaguely haunted.

"Now don't think this was some gay thing, 'cause it wasn't. He wasn't interested in me anymore than I was interested in him. But we'd grown up together, sort of grown apart through the years simply because he was more athletic than I was, but we'd been friends. He'd been the one who found me in the bathroom, called for help, saved me. There he was, saving me again. Calling me for ice cream in the middle of March. I expected it to be a trick but went anyway, figuring I could just end everything when I got home. I just had this tiny bit of hope, that maybe, just maybe, someone cared."

He moved to the other side of the stage, making eye contact with people in the crowd as he spoke. "Now there wasn't some grand revelation or age-old conversation about how my life was important, and he was glad to have saved me. No. We ate ice cream and talked about anime, of all things. I told him how I hated anime 'cause of all the big-breasted women in skimpy clothes, expecting him to call me a fag, but he laughed and told me that was only some of it. He told me about some of his favorites, which were more about acceptance than boobage. Even admitted to liking something called *Fruits Basket*." He laughed and smiled at Adam. Adam was sure he was blushing.

"I thought, man, this guy has to be gay to like something called *Fruits Basket*. You seen it?" he asked the crowd. Some said yes, some said no. "It's about a girl who loses her parents and decides not to burden anyone, so she goes to live in the woods. She doesn't knock herself off or grovel in the sorrow of her lot. No, she sets forth to do the best she can and become the best person she can be. It doesn't hurt that she meets some hot guys on the way. But while she's not the most popular girl in school, she does find acceptance, not only from others, but for herself. She also teaches others to accept themselves. I watched the whole damn series, which, if you know anything about anime, means a lot.

"So he told me about this series and was so animated and happy that I couldn't help but feel lighter around him. Like maybe things weren't all bad if someone like this could exist. I found out some interesting things about him that night. Like the fact that he doesn't have a Facebook page, never surfs the Internet for porn, and never looked at someone else with judgment." He nodded his head. "I know, right? Wow. He's a lot like that girl from the anime. Changing people without really trying. Changing the world by just being a little different himself."

He waved his hand. "I drove him home, and he got out of the car, a big smile on his face, and said, 'See you tomorrow, right?' And I nodded dumbly, like sure, whatever. When I got home, there was a text with his schedule, showing that we had the same lunch hour. And he asked to eat with me. I couldn't believe it. Someone wanted to eat with me, the fag who just got his shit kicked in the boys' bathroom. But when I got to the lunchroom that day, after enduring all the stares and the total silence from my peers, he was sitting with a bunch of jocks. Some of those very same jocks who had hurt me. At that moment it was like the ultimate betrayal. Here I was, still alive and suffering, hopes high only to be dashed. But then he turned, smiled, and waved me over."

Bas sat down on the edge of the stage, staring out at everyone. "When I sat down next to him, no one said a damn thing. Those asshole jocks wouldn't meet my eyes. No one got up from the table in a huff, and it was okay to sit there and just talk, just be me. Now of course, in time, the teasing returned, but this boy had become this sort of shield to me. He wasn't all that popular or big and scary-looking, but what he had that kept the jerks back was confidence."

The map came back up with all the faces. "One little word can defeat the bullies and stop the needless death. Confidence. Now you all look at me like I'm nuts. 'Bas,' you tell me, 'I'm in high school. No high school kid has confidence.' But that's not true. One does—one did. Someone tried to take that away from him on Friday night, and they failed. It's not about who's biggest, strongest, or even the smartest. Life is about moving forward, being who you are. If you're too afraid to walk down the hall, too afraid to speak out and be yourself, you're being held back." He motioned to the map. "Is that where you want to be? Is that all that's left for you? I say no. See, this same boy, who always stood up for me without even knowing it, had sort of been coasting through his life on autopilot. You know what happens when you're on autopilot?"

He nodded again. "Life throws you a curve. His confidence wavered. Everyone surged in like vultures to tear apart the wounded creature he'd become. Only he brushed them off and got right back up again."

The picture with the bully came back up again. "I graduate this year. I know I owe a lot to my friend. I'm going to a great college, have big plans for the future, hope to someday find someone who accepts me for who I am so I can spend my life growing old with them. In twenty years I will look back and think, wow, those bullies really weren't a big deal; but that one guy, him I'll remember. Who do you want to be? The guy who stood by and let it happen or was even bullying others, or the guy who stood up and made an impact?"

Bas got up and made his way back to the podium. "Thanks for letting me speak to you. Now Principal O'Brien has a few announcements."

Everyone clapped, though Adam felt a rumbling discord of unease from everyone around him. He would have to talk to Bas about the saintlike role he'd placed on Adam's head. The principal stepped up to the mic. "Thank you, Sebastian. Now, a few general announcements. First, we have a no-tolerance policy for bullying; that means name-calling, notes pushed in lockers, shoving, or property damage will all result in immediate repercussions. We have, unfortunately, been a bit slack with these rules. However, there will now be faculty added to the hallways between classes to prevent these issues. All students should feel safe while attending school."

He paused, cleared his throat, and then continued. "You may have noticed that some of your peers are missing from school today. We have suspended eleven students and expelled three others."

Adam sucked in a deep breath. Had Nate been expelled? Who else?

"No tolerance means *no* tolerance. Shove someone in the hall and you're suspended. Shout things at them, throw things at them, write a nasty note, and don't think it won't get to me. We spent a good part of the weekend comparing handwriting on hateful notes with the handwriting on term papers. Do you all understand that this is not negotiable?"

There was a murmur of consent throughout the auditorium.

"Good. Now go back to class."

Everyone rose en masse like some zombie exodus. Adam waited a moment, hoping for a word with Bas, but freshmen were already making their way in to fill the room. Bas waved him away, mouthing "Later."

By lunch all of the meetings were finished. Adam walked through the lunchroom, searching the room like everyone else to discover who was missing. Nate was gone, and so were Hank and Jonah. He glanced at the lunch options and wrinkled his nose at the idea of spaghetti from a giant vat. Maybe Ru would take him somewhere for lunch.

Bas met him at the door, and they headed outside to find Ru, bundled up like an Eskimo, sitting on a giant blanket with a box of pizza in front of him. "Maybe I should go back in," Bas suggested. "I don't want to interrupt."

Adam rolled his eyes. "As if anything is going to happen on school grounds."

Ru smiled at them both as they settled onto the blanket too. The pizza was from Dimitri's, of course, and loaded with so much it was more than enough for the three of them. "Going to have to run later to work this off," Ru told them.

Bas shook his head.

"So, Axelrod," Adam said, smiling while he thought about his day so far. "I'm your hero, huh?"

"Maybe."

Adam threw Ru a sneaky smile and wink, then turned to Bas. "There's this guy in Advisory who was asking about you."

"In a good way, or a bad way?"

"A good way." Adam proceeded to tell his friend about Dustin, the guy who was apparently pining for Bas. Maybe things would work out okay after all.

CHAPTER 23

BY THE time the weekend rolled around again, Ru couldn't wait to have Adam all for himself. He was beginning to believe he had to enroll at Northern to spend more than a few hours with the guy at a time. He and Adam still ran most days after school. It was Adam's writing for the newspaper that kept him late most days, pushing their training and dinner back. Most nights they ended up sitting on the Corbins' couch, too tired to do anything other than hold hands and snuggle a little.

But Friday night was their date. Dimitri had cleared out the whole restaurant for them. It would be private and nonthreatening. A cameraman would meet them there to take pictures of the two of them, and Ru had already agreed to answer most of the questions Ryan Hart had sent him ahead of time. What Ru didn't plan for was date-ready Adam.

Ru appeared at the Corbin's house just after five, hoping for a leisurely ride to his uncle's restaurant with a little snogging on the way. But when Adam stepped onto the stairway, all reasonable intelligence left Ru's head. The blond wore a bright blue-and-green striped sweater that hugged him just right, showing off his great shoulders and slim waist. Then there were the jeans—pale washed but still darker than what most kids wore. When Adam had tried them on, Ru insisted he buy them. In those jeans, Adam's long, strong legs and thighs led to a perfect little butt, all outlined by a perfect cut. His blond hair had been brushed to a silky shine that Ru longed to run his fingers through.

"Do I look okay?" Adam asked. "You have a funny look on your face."

"Um, wow?" Ru tried and failed miserably to say something intelligent. When Adam stood in front of him, meeting his gaze eye to eye, he had to blink a few times to refocus his brain. "Okay, you can't have pictures of you taken like this."

"It's that bad?" Adam asked, looking alarmed.

"No, you look that good. People are going to try to steal you from me the second they see you." Ru pouted.

Adam laughed. "Seriously. Are you ready to go? We have an interview with some bigwig writer guy."

Ru shook his head, finding his boyfriend so hard to believe sometimes. "You do know you're dating a guy who's won Grammy awards and stuff, right?"

"Yeah, but you're kissing me. He's sort of examining me."

"Better not be. Only I get to examine you."

Adam blushed. Ru grabbed his hand and tugged him out to the car. At the restaurant, most of the tables had been cleared out so the set for the photos could be built. Dimitri stood off to the side, beaming at Ru like a proud father. Ru couldn't help but smile back. His uncle gave him a bone-crushing hug before letting the cameraman take over. It was going to be Ru's first shoot ever without makeup, without the couture that made up his rock-star persona. In fact, he and Adam decided they would be doing this without shoes or socks.

Something about having his feet bare just made him feel exposed. In Adam's opinion, this interview was meant to expose them both for whom and what they were. And he wanted it to be as real as possible. At the time Ru had agreed, thinking it would be no big deal. But as he sat under the heavy lights with Adam, he worried about what the camera would reveal. They'd take a hundred shots and only use two or three. That was the way of things, but while Ru was tense and struggled to work with the cameraman, Adam did exactly what was asked, even cracked a few jokes to get Ru laughing.

"Seriously, did you hear the one about the people putting a fence around the graveyard?" Adam asked, his expression one of utter seriousness. "People were just dying to get in."

"Wow, that was awful." Ru laughed, though, because Adam was laughing, and he was sort of infectious that way. There was a lot of hand holding and a few tiny kisses, but finally the photo shoot was over, and they got to make their way to the table where Ryan Hart and his partner waited. Adam gripped his hand tightly but smiled freely at the men, even offering to shake their hands.

Ryan motioned them to the table that had been set up for them with flowers and candles and all the things romantic dates were supposed to be. Only, of course, theirs had an interview included.

"Don't be nervous," Adam whispered to Ru. "I've been e-mailing Ryan back and forth all week. He likes my articles, and he's really nice. So let's just eat and let the conversation go where it goes. No more hiding, right?"

Ru stared at his boyfriend, more amazed every second they spent together. "I've got nothing to hide. Though I am sort of a jealous boyfriend." He glanced at Ryan. "Hopefully that little fact can be made clear in your article?"

Ryan smiled. "Of course."

SAM KADENCE has always dreamed about being someone else, somewhere else. With very little musical talent, Sam decided the only way to make those dreams come true was to try everything from cosplay at the local anime conventions to writing novels about pretending to run away to become a musician.

Sam has a Bachelor's degree in Creative Writing, sells textbooks for a living, enjoys taking photographs of Asian Ball Joint Dolls to tell more stories, and has eclectic taste in music from J-pop to rock and country. All of which finds its way into the books eventually.

Facebook: https://www.facebook.com/SamKadence

Also from SAM KADENCE

EVOLUTION
SAM KADENCE

http://www.harmonyinkpress.com

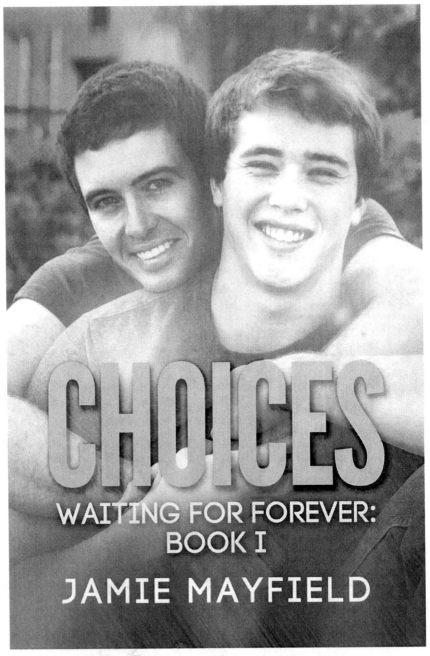

CHOICES

WAITING FOR FOREVER:
BOOK I

JAMIE MAYFIELD

Also from H<small>ARMONY</small> I<small>NK</small> P<small>RESS</small>

DESTINY

WAITING FOR FOREVER:
BOOK II

JAMIE MAYFIELD

http://www.harmonyinkpress.com

DETERMINATION

WAITING FOR FOREVER:
BOOK III

JAMIE MAYFIELD

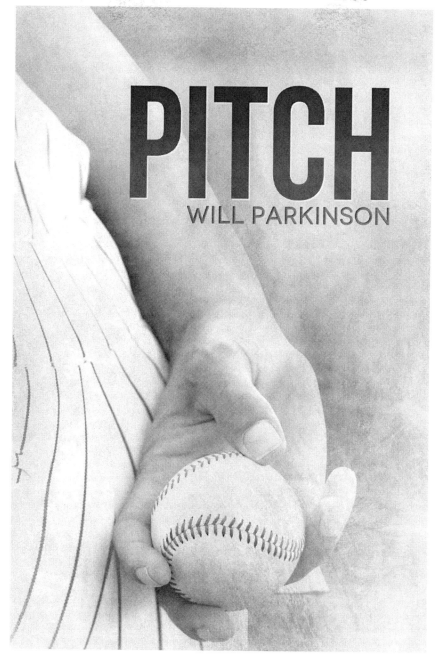

PITCH

WILL PARKINSON

Harmony Ink

3 9384 00111 8218   7/16

CPSIA information can be obtained
at www.ICGtesting.com
Printed in the USA
FFOW01n0939210616
25204FF